Hard and Ruthless

Lock Down Publications and Ca$h
Presents
Hard and Ruthless
A Novel by *Von Wiley Hall*

Hard and Ruthless

Lock Down Publications
P.O. Box 944
Stockbridge, Ga 30281
www.lockdownpublications.com

Copyright 2021 Von Wiley Hall
Hard and Ruthless

First Edition January 2021
Printed in the United States of America

Lock Down Publications
Like our page on Facebook: Lock Down Publications @
www.facebook.com/lockdownpublications.ldp
Cover design and layout by: **Dynasty Cover Me**
Book interior design by: **Shawn Walker**
Edited by: **Leondra Williams**

Von Wiley Hall

Stay Connected with Us!

Text **LOCKDOWN** to 22828 to stay up-to-date with new releases, sneak peaks, contests and more…

Thank you!

Submission Guideline.

Submit the first three chapters of your completed manuscript to ldpsubmissions@gmail.com, subject line: Your book's title. The manuscript must be in a .doc file and sent as an attachment. Document should be in Times New Roman, double spaced and in size 12 font. Also, provide your synopsis and full contact information. If sending multiple submissions, they must each be in a separate email.

Have a story but no way to send it electronically? You can still submit to LDP/Ca$h Presents. Send in the first three chapters, written or typed, of your completed manuscript to:

LDP: Submissions Dept
P.O. Box 944
Stockbridge, Ga 30281

DO NOT send original manuscript. Must be a duplicate.

Provide your synopsis and a cover letter containing your full contact information.

Thanks for considering LDP and Ca$h Presents.

DEDICATION

This book is dedicated to Harold (Lil' Cheez) Edwards Jr.and Demarius (Dee) Arnez Wiley. May God continue to bless you. Until we meet again, I love you both. Fly high, fam. R.I.P.

SPECIAL DEDICATION

Ms. Brenda L. Thomas, thank you for being such an inspiration to my life. It's so strange how God places people in your life for all of the right reasons with no strings attached. You have taught me patience in this writing process. You are such an idol in the writing industry. Your books are awesome reads and you are by far one of the most talented female writers in the industry. You have been here for me since day one, listening to me as I vented concerning my cartoon and children's books. I owe you dearly for your effortless help and your dedication. You have seen something special within me from the start and you've pushed me to complete my journey. I love you unconditionally for being there and never leaving me in my trying times. Such a wonderful, heaven-sent angel. I thank you for continuing to manage me, market my ideas...for your honesty and loyalty. You will always be in my heart and remember...when our project blows up, I will continue to be the same person that I am now, and will effortlessly look out for the people who have helped me along the way and the ones who are less fortunate.

ACKNOWLEDGEMENTS

As, always, I must first acknowledge and thank GOD, because without him, none of this would be possible. The ability to tell stories with so much creativity blows my mind more and more as I continue this journey. THANK YOU SO MUCH...YOU ARE GREAT AND WORTHY TO BE PRAISED.

I would like to thank God for keeping me through all of life's ups and downs, and for giving me the most beautiful children I could ever ask for. To MY GOLDEN GIFTS: Ashley, Ashton, Deryka, Jamie, Haley and Brooklyn.

And to my four GOLDEN NUGGET Grandkids: T.J., Tristan, Karter and Kameron. The reason why I am going so hard is because of you.

I would like to thank Bobby Bates and Derrick Hall. You never dropped the plate when it came down to taking care of your responsibilities. I love you both unconditionally.

To my father, James Loren Moton...Thanks for giving me life. You are the world's greatest dad. I love you.

To my mother...Rest in peace; my angel.

I would like to give a loud shout out to my only sibling...RAYMOND WILEY. You are the best man, father and brother anyone could ever ask for. I love you so much. I am so proud of you for just being a man, and doing everything that our grandfather instilled in you. You are always here for me, and there hasn't been one time that I have ever asked you for anything and didn't receive it. Remember that you are the gift that my mother gave me. I LOVE YOU TO THE MOON AND BACK!

God, I ask you to protect my family and continue to give them grace and mercy. To the WILEY FAMILY: Wow, what can I say. Never seen a family so dedicated to loving one another and taking care of each other. All I was ever taught was how to love and help those in need. I know that life dealt me a bad had a few times...but as Jamie Loren Hall would say...I just played the cards that I was given. All I ever wanted in life was happiness and peace. A special shout-out to my Aunt PeeWee, Aunt Brenda, Aunt Debra, Aunt Sandra, Aunt Bonnie, Aunt Sylvia, Aunt Cynthia and Aunt Pearl...Uncle J.B. (Junebug), Uncle Dennis, Uncle Alvin and Uncle Luke. I Love You All.

To Dorothy Smith (Momma D), and Linda Shannon (Stixx)...thanks for reading my manuscripts over and over and over again and for giving me positive feedback.

Sharon Hendricks, thanks for always keeping it real and for being my best friends for all of these years. May God continue to shine his light upon you and your family.

7

Sandie Wiley Atkins, Stacey Wiley, Timethia Nichols, Chantae Thomas, Orenthal Butler (JoJo), Marcus Wiley, Felecia Brooks, Angela Brooks, Raymond Brooks Jr., Chris McCants and Asia...What up fam?

To my only nephew, Jaylun Wiley...love you.

Layla Grace, Jeremiah and Harlon...what up?

Vantel Atkins...thought I forgot you, huh?

J.B. Wiley Sr. and Mattie Mae Wiley R.I.P. Best grandparents ever.

Thanks to Mrs. Robinson, my factory manager and the entire CSR Staff, Mrs. Richardson, Mr. Moore, Mr. Harper, Mr. Broadwater, Ms. Pierson, and Mr. Price. You've paved the way for so many. Thanks for your support and your kindness. To my coach Stacy Merell, Rita Peak, Tiffany Arnold, Juanita Lawson, (Star) Kizer, Donna Moonda, Rebecca Christie, Kirsten Henry, Renita Miller, Angie Smith and to the top dog Cathy Wood and you too Robin Chaney.

Mrs. Harvey, Ms. Lassiter, Mr. Thomas and Mr. Escaffi, thanks for all that you have done and all that you continue to do.

YOU ARE THE GREATEST TEAM EVER!

Patti Siacca, dawg, you the coolest ever.

Jenna Martin, Da Savage, Unk, Spoon, Stacey Bond what up?

Camilla Whitaker and Johnya Franklin...What up peeps?

Kathea Adams (City) and Naomi Zaccardi what it do?

I saved the best for last, a special shout out to CA$H and the entire LDP Staff, thank you so much for allowing me to be a part of the team. You took a chance on me and I'ma do the damn thang!

Let's get this money!

MASK UP PEOPLE...THE COVID IS REAL!

Hard and Ruthless

Chapter One

Rhapsodee despised going to the super Walmart with a passion, but it was the only place she could shop and get everything she needed. After she paid for her items, she pushed her buggy toward the door and without looking up, she accidentally ran into the finest piece of chocolate she had ever seen.

"I'm so sorry," she apologized. The sight of his caramel skin laced with tattoos turned her on immediately. She quickly erased her lustful thoughts since she was a married woman. The way he looked at her, put her in a trance.

"If you wasn't so damn sexy, I would have given you pure hell, but all I want is them digits, so you can make it up to me," the man spoke in his sexy Denzel voice, causing her pussy juices to flow immediately and soak her panties.

Get it together Rhapsodee. Don't let that nigga run pickup lines on you she thought to herself.

"If I wasn't a married woman, I would probably take you up on your offer, but since I am, seems like you're out of luck," Rhapsodee smiled and flashed her ring.

"Man, fuck that nigga, and if that's the shit he gave you, then he doesn't deserve you no way."

His comment insulted Rhapsodee, and she knew it was time to get the fuck out of Walmart's parking lot. That nigga was bold as hell, but Rhapsodee couldn't let him just stand there and talk shit about her ole' man. She loved her ring, fuck what he said.

"Fuck you!" She brushed past him, rolling her fake lashes.

"Nigga gave you a cracker jack ring."

Rhapsodee flipped him the middle finger and went on her way.

"I'm just being honest shawty, with your sexy ass. The name is Black. Remember it because you gonna be mine as soon as he fucks up, ya heard me?"

Rhapsodee heard everything he said. She made her way to her black on black Range Rover and smiled at the plans she had made for her twenty-eighth birthday, which was also their four-year anniversary.

Hard and Ruthless

It was a cold ass January day, so she turned the heat on high and embraced its warmth. Something made Rhapsodee look through her rearview mirror. She saw Black walking across the parking lot. It seemed as if he felt her because they instantly locked eyes. Even though he pissed her off, she let her feelings fly past her shoulder because she knew she would never see his arrogant ass ever again and that was a damn good thing.

Rhapsodee made her way to her condo and noticed her phone ringing. She pulled it out of her Prada purse and saw that it was her cousin, Leah.

"Hey Leah," she said.

"What up bitch?" replied Leah.

"Just left funky ass Walmart, heading in the house now".

"Two things, you going out with me Saturday night and I need that beige dress I left at your place. So, I'll be there in a few to get it."

"Hoe I ain't..."

Before Rhapsodee could say anything, Leah had hung up.

"This bitch got some nerve," Rhapsodee mumbled under her breath.

Rhapsodee rode the rest of the way home listening to Cardi B's debut album. Even though she had heard *Bodak Yellow* a million times before, she still didn't skip it when it sounded through the speakers. The album was a smasher. Rhapsodee never found time to listen to it in its entirety, but she made time for Cardi today. About twenty minutes later, she turned into The Vineyard at Piedmont. She smiled when she saw both of Swerve's whips in their assigned spaces. She figured that he would still be at work but was pleasantly surprised because she could use some of his bomb ass sex at that moment. Working as a traveling nurse was very rewarding, but oftentimes, it would be stressful and draining.

Rhapsodee grabbed a couple of bags, then got out and headed for the door. When she finally made it, she inserted her key in the knob, then twisted it. She didn't hear it click, so that meant the door wasn't locked. Although the neighborhood was lavish, locking the door was always natural. She wondered why Swerve didn't lock it.

11

Rhapsodee shrugged it off and made her way inside. The sound of R. Kelly's *Sex Me* was coming from the surround sound. She put the bags on the table and couldn't wait to be wrapped up in Swerve's arms. The thought of him beating up her sugar walls made her smile.

"Hey babe, what…" Rhapsodee's sentence was cut short after she saw her husband's dick down the throat of a tramp bitch she had never seen before. "What the fuck?" Rhapsodee screamed and lunged forward.

Chapter Two

The heat from Yoshi's mouth on Swerve's dick had him feeling so good, he never heard Rhapsodee open the door. He snapped back to reality when he heard screams coming from both Rhapsodee and Yoshi. Rhapsodee pulled Yoshi by her raggedy ass lace front, and sucker punched that hoe smack dead in her face. It took Swerve's dick one point two seconds to shrivel back up. He knew he should have pulled Rhapsodee off of Yoshi, but instead, he grabbed his boxers and put them on. He didn't know that Rhapsodee was a fighter, but she was whooping Yoshi's ass like Ike did Tina.

"Hold up baby, it ain't what it looks like!"

"Fuck you mean, it ain't what it looks like? Ain't shit wrong with these two muthafuckin' eyes. The hoe was eating ya dick and yo ugly ass was enjoying it. Don't touch me, nigga. And you, you think I'ma let you bring some trailer park ass thot up in here and let you fuck like you got it like that? Nigga let me the fuck go, because I got something for your ass too," yelled Rhapsodee.

Rhapsodee was stronger than Swerve had given her credit for. She slipped straight through his grip, scratching him on his arm with her fingernails in the process.

Swerve watched as Yoshi tried to escape out the door, but before she could leave, Leah walked in.

"Fuck y'all got going on up in here?"

"This nigga gettin' his dick sucked by this trashy ass bitch, and I'm finna body bag both of their asses."

After she said that, Swerve watched Leah go ham on Yoshi.

"And you nigga, the fuck you playing with Rhap for? Your ass ain't shit."

Leah reached up and hit Swerve upside his head, and then her and Rhapsodee tag teamed him and commenced to whooping his ass so bad, he had no choice but surrender and leave.

He saw the hurt in Rhapsodee's eyes and decided he'd give her time to cool off. He jumped in his Denali and sped off so fast, he almost ran over Yoshi as she hobbled down the street, limping with one red bottom on and the other one was only God knows where.

Swerve headed towards Dudley's, pulling up fifteen minutes later. He parked and went inside. Swerve walked in and copped a seat. He noticed a sexy ass bartender smiling and walking his way. He wanted to flirt with her, but with what happened earlier, he knew he had to keep things on ice.

"Hi handsome, what can I get ya?"

"Let me get a Grand Marnier with coke on the rocks."

"Coming right up," she flirted and slung her hips to the bar.

As soon as she turned her back, he felt his phone vibrating. He assumed it was Yoshi calling again, but when he noticed it was his homie, Big Posse, he answered it.

"Whaddup my nigga?"

"Shit. What happened? Yoshi called crying and shit," Big Posse complained.

"Shit's wild, man. I'on know. One minute we're spending time together and the next, Rhapsodee came through out of nowhere, tearing shit up. She scared the fuck outta me."

Swerve downed his drink as soon as the bartender sat it in front of him. He knew he had to now deal with Big Posse's push back, so he was preparing himself for it. In the past when Swerve and Yoshi argued, she would wait a few days before she would tell her brother anything. Now Swerve wished he would have ignored his call. He listened as Big Posse cussed him out. He was dead ass wrong and he knew it.

"I told y'all to cut this fuck shit years ago. LEAVE MY SISTER THE FUCK ALONE NIGGA." Big Posse yelled, then hung up before Swerve could respond.

Big Posse had been Swerve's boy for as long as he could remember. They went all the way back to second grade. When Swerve and Yoshi first started having sex, Big Posse was furious. He and Swerve had a fight that almost ended their friendship. Big Posse didn't approve of their relationship.

"You look like your whole world just blew up," the bartender said as she sat another drink in front of him.

"Shit. Ms. Lady, you don't know the half of it," he said as the liquor began to take over.

14

Swerve picked up his iPhone and tried calling his wife back. It rang and went straight to voicemail. At least she hadn't blocked him yet. He put the phone down and started venting to Ms. So So Sexy.

After a minute, he got up determined to get home. He staggered a little bit.

"You shouldn't drive in your condition," the bartender said.

"I-I-I'm good," he stuttered.

"Let me help you to your whip, then you can relax there for a minute," she pulled him along.

When Swerve woke up a few hours later, he was in an unfamiliar place and began to panic. Last thing he remembered he was having a few rounds at the bar, then his head began to pound.

"You up, Mr. Sleepy Head?" a voice asked.

"The fuck?" Swerve mumbled as a light in his head popped on, noticing the bartender from the bar.

"You were too drunk to drive, so I drove you here. Your trucks parked outside."

Shit started to come back and at that moment, he wondered how he allowed himself to get that drunk. He needed to get home before Rhapsodee was done with his ass for good. The bartender looked so good, that his dick began to bulge through his pants. He knew right then it was time to dip.

"Sorry about all this. This shit ain't never popped off like this before." He stood on his fee still a bit wasted.

He locked eyes with the beautiful woman whose name he didn't know and saw her smirk as she looked at his hard print.

"My keys?"

"Oh yeah," she replied.

He grabbed his keys and headed for the door. He wanted to know her name, but he made the smart choice to ignore it and leave. He cranked up his Denali and prayed the entire ride home that Rhapsodee had cooled down.

He pulled up to their condo and just sat there. Swerve grabbed his iPhone and clicked on his messages. Yoshi had called a few times, but he never answered. He clicked on the text she sent him.

15

Yoshi: SWERVE, YOU HAVE FUCKED OVER ME FOR THE LAST MUTHAFUCKIN TIME. I THOUGHT YOU LEFT THAT CRAZY ASS BITCH. JUST KNOW THE GAMES HAVE JUST BEGUN, PHUCK BOI.

Chapter Three

"Bitch, this what you not gone do. You ain't about to cry over this scum ass nigga. It's time to do you ma," expressed Leah.

"You don't understand, I love this muthafucka."

"Look, I know you do, but these hoe ass niggas ain't loyal. How many times I gotta tell you this? I think the only reason why he is with you is because you're successful, but that's neither here nor there."

Rhapsodee never had proof of Swerve ever cheating on her, but the nigga always looked sneaky.

"You think he cheated on me before?" asked Rhapsodee

"Shit, why you asking me? You gotta ask him."

"I know you tired of hearing my bullshit. Let me get your dress so you can go. I think I'm gonna stay in tonight."

"Suit yourself, but you know I'm always here for you right?"

"Yeah, I know. Here's your dress."

They hugged for a few minutes.

Leah finally left and headed for her apartment. Leah already knew that Rhapsodee wasn't going to go out with her, and with the shit Swerve pulled, the chances really vanished. It was a good thing she was really going to kick it with E-Love, so she didn't need to call her homegirl City, who would ride out with her at the drop of a beat.

About eleven fifteen, Leah admired herself in her full-length mirror and snapped a couple of pictures. Her skin tone was a cocoa brown, and she could stand with the baddest bitches. Red was Leah's favorite color and she sported it often. With her natural curly hair flowing down her back, if you didn't know Leah, you would think it was weave. Running track in high school helped her to develop legs most would pay for. She was five foot eight inches tall and could have easily been a model. Leah posted pictures and videos on Facebook and Instagram and then dipped out. A short while later, Leah pulled into the parking lot of Big Daddy's and parked her Range.

The parking lot was full. Big Daddy's was one of the hang out spots in Atlanta that was popping through the week. Leah made her way in the club and Cardi B and Bruno Mars *Tease Me* sounded through the speakers. She made her way to the VIP section and the first person she saw was E-Love. Some hoe ass thot was giving him a lap dance. Leah was glad they weren't official because she would have been dishing out the second beat down for the day. Leah knew E-Love had that bank, but she wasn't sure if he was worth more than he portrayed. It really wasn't her concern as long as he continued giving her major ends. They had been kicking it for a year, but she guarded her feelings. She knew the type of nigga E-Love was and she wasn't about to get caught up in his shit.

"Excuse you, this nigga is mine for tonight!" Leah pushed the chick off E-Love and took her position.

"Who the fucks this hoe?" the girl screamed.

"Hold up, chill out Lil Mama," E-Love intervened as Leah was about to check ole' girl.

Leah noticed the look on the girl's face, and knew she wasn't about to back down, but after a minute she slowly walked away.

"You love entertaining these lil bitches, don't you? You gon' fuck around and get somebody fucked the fuck up!" she whispered in E-Love's ear.

"Put that lil hot ass pussy on me and don't worry about them hoes."

Right then, Usher's *Trading Places* filled the club. By the time the song ended, Leah could tell that E-Love was ready to fuck. Just as she was about to grind on his dick, shots rang out and he pushed her to the floor.

"Stay here and don't move," instructed E-Love.

E-Love was gone, and his boys were right behind him. A few minutes later, the lights came on and everybody scattered. Just as Leah got up to step out of the VIP section, she felt someone tap her shoulder. When she turned around, she was face to face with the same bitch who was giving E-Love his lap dance.

Leah saw the bitch taking off her shoes, and before she could stand up straight, Leah stepped right up and two pieced her in her

18

ugly ass face. One thing about fucking a bitch up is that you had to stay ready, so you wouldn't have to get ready. As soon as Leah had ole' girl in the headlock, E-Love picked her up and carried her out of the club. Once inside the car, outta nowhere, glass shattered, and they ducked.

"The fuck?" they said in unison.

When they finally looked up, they saw it was the bitch from the club.

"Go get that hoe," said E-Love.

Von Wiley Hall

Chapter Four

E-Love got out of his car and watched Leah beat the fuck out of Simone. A crowd had already formed, and people were recording the fight left and right. He looked over his right shoulder and saw one of the security dudes that he was cool with. Judging by the look that the dude gave him, E-Love knew it was only a matter of time before someone called the cops. He made his way towards Leah, and once again, he picked her little ass up and carried her back to the car. He drove away and a few minutes later, he heard her fussing about breaking a nail. He was trying his best to keep it cool so that the cop he had just passed, wouldn't turn around and follow them.

As soon as they were in the clear, E-Love let out the breath he didn't know he'd been holding. Atlanta police were known to be assholes and he had already had a few indirect run-ins with them but had been doing his best to stay off their radar. He didn't need those type of problems, and he definitely didn't want to use the connections that he had until it was absolutely necessary. He navigated towards Leah's apartment, but made a pit stop at the Shell gas station so that he could grab some cigars. She had finally got quiet and he was glad because arguing wasn't on his mind. He was ready to dip inside of her and fuck the shit out of her juicy pussy.

"Get me a peach Fanta," she rolled her eyes and told him before he got out of the car.

The feistiness in her voice made his dick hard and she didn't even know it. If he was the settling down type, Leah would actually be the one that he wifed up, but since he was what he liked to call a "free spirit", he didn't even bother lying to her. They had been kicking it for a little while, but he really cared about her more than he was willing to admit.

E-Love made his way inside and went straight to the back where the drinks were and grabbed Leah's soda. Since she liked Sour Cream-n-Onion chips, he picked up a bag before he made it to the counter. E-Love asked for some Swishers, paid for all of his shit, and then turned to leave. He bumped into Simone's lil thot ass friend that had been trying to fuck him on the low for the longest. He knew

21

that she had to be alone and was about to shoot her shot, but he excused himself and left before she could even get started.

"You gon' stop running one day," she called out to him, but E-Love kept walking.

He hopped back behind the wheel and took off. Leah appeared to be viewing snaps or some shit on her phone. E-Love was the type that wasn't into social media. He had pages but rarely used them. He knew a lot just because of all the other females he fucked with.

"I thought we were going to your place tonight?" Leah said once he turned into her complex.

"Your place was closer, baby."

"You lucky I need some dick. Now hurry up because I just got a text, and I gotta go in a couple hours early tomorrow for a meeting." Leah got out, fussing.

One of the things he liked most about her was that she held herself down. It made E-Love give her shit because she never asked. Leah worked as a business consultant, and she was passionate about her job. He loved to hear her talk about helping people achieve their goals. When it was time for him to turn clean, he would probably use her to help him get some legit shit off the ground. E-Love got out and followed Leah inside. She stripped out of her dress as soon as they entered her apartment. Just looking at her ass made his dick grow.

"I broke a fuckin' nail because of yo ass," Leah fussed as he walked into her room.

"I got you, bae," E-Love replied as he walked over and picked her up.

He threw her on the bed and started fondling with her breasts. Her moans escaped her lips when he started sucking on her right nipple. He slipped his fingers inside of her white satin panties, as he felt her wetness drip. He peeled off her panties, slipped on a magnum and slowly eased inside her pussy.

"Oh shit," she screamed.

"Feels good, don't it, baby?"

E-Love lifted her legs and slowly stroked her deeper. Shit felt so good to him. He went crazy as she clenched her muscles around his dick. He couldn't control the feeling any longer. His nut was so strong, he damn near had a heart attack.

"Damn, that pussy is good," spat E-Love.

"Exactly, but if it was so good, then why I gotta be fighting all these hoes?" asked Leah.

"Come on baby. Why you gotta ruin the moment?"

"I mean you don't want me fucking other niggas, right?"

The shit she said made E-Love stop and think. Leah wasn't brave enough to fuck another nigga, and if she did, he was gonna show her a side of him that she has never seen. She was his, and that meant by any means necessary.

Von Wiley Hall

Chapter Five

When Leah left, Rhapsodee told herself to get it together. She walked to the kitchen to get her something to drink. She realized that she didn't get the rest of the groceries out of her Range. She went out and grabbed the rest of her items. Visualizing another bitches mouth around Swerve's dick kept popping in her mind. She was torn but didn't want to divorce Swerve's inconsiderate ass.

Rhapsodee's cell phone rang as she put up her groceries. She knew it was Swerve by his ringtone. Her favorite song, *Tease Me* by Guy was playing in her ear. By the time she answered the call, Swerve was walking through the door.

"We need to talk, baby. Just hear me out," Swerve pleaded.

Rhapsodee didn't know if he was spitting bullshit or not, but she told him she was listening.

"Look, I was wrong and I'm sorry. What I did was fucked up. I never had sex with Yoshi baby. She just sucked my dick. Shit will never happen again, I promise."

Rhapsodee closed her eyes and took a deep breath.

"So, if you walked in on another nigga eating my pussy, would you take me back?" she asked.

"Huh?"

"If you can huh, you can hear."

"Yes, cause I love you."

"Swerve, you're so full of shit and you know damned well, it wouldn't go that easy," said Rhapsodee.

"Baby I want our marriage to work. I love you," Swerve said, coming closer.

"The best thing for you to do is to leave *now* Swerve!"

"I ain't going no muthafuckin' where."

"Oh yeah muthafucka," snapped Rhapsodee. "Just have your ass sitting right there when I get back, that's what you do. I'ma show you that I ain't playing with you today."

Rhapsodee made it to her nightstand, opened the drawer, and pulled out her 45. As soon as Swerve walked through her bedroom door, she pulled the trigger.

Von Wiley Hall

Chapter Six

"Damn," Swerve screamed and hit the floor while grabbing his leg.

"Oh my God! I didn't mean to shoot you, baby. I'm so sorry. I meant to scare you. Oh my God!" Rhapsodee sobbed hysterically and rushed over to him. "I gotta call 911," Rhapsodee became petrified.

"Baby, no. Wait, we gotta think of what to say," Swerve panicked.

He was in excruciating pain, but he didn't want Rhapsodee getting into any trouble with the law. Her shooting him was probably going to be his ticket out of the doghouse and he was damn sure going to take advantage of the situation. Swerve saw the hurt, pain and regret etched on Rhapsodee's face. He couldn't believe that she had shot his ass, but then again, he was grateful she didn't grab the gun earlier and kill him on sight.

"You're hurting. Oh my God, we gotta do something," she cried.

"I'll be okay. Grab some towels right quick," Swerve told her.

Rhapsodee ran to get the towels and made it back speedily. She tied a towel around his leg causing Swerve to scream out in agony because the shit really did hurt.

"I'm sorry. We gotta get you to the hospital. Come on, let me help you up."

Swerve didn't protest that time around even though he had only been shot in the leg, the blood hadn't stopped squirting out and the pain was real. They made it out of the house with him leaning most of his weight on Rhapsodee, but she was taking it like a champ. Since his keys were the first ones in sight, Rhapsodee grabbed those and Swerve hoped like hell there wasn't anything in his whip that would make her shoot him again and then really kill his ass. She hit the alarm to his black Challenger and the headlights flashed and the alarm beeped simultaneously. Rhapsodee made her way around to the passenger's side, opened the door and then placed a blanket that she had grabbed and other towels on the seat before she helped Swerve inside.

When she got in, she cranked up and sped away. She drove away so fast that Swerve's head jerked backwards. Rhapsodee asked him over and over how he was feeling. He told her that he was fine, but he actually began to feel a little faint.

"Tell them you thought I was breaking in and you shot me. You weren't trying to shoot to kill, just to scare someone and you panicked and brought me to the hospital."

"You think that's gonna work?"

"Yeah, but hurry up 'cause I feel weak," Swerve mumbled. He heard Rhapsodee call his name, but he drifted off into complete darkness.

When Swerve woke up, the bright lights caused him to close his eyes right back. He opened them back a few minutes later and then tried to sit up.

"You're awake. Thank you, Jesus. How are you?" Rhapsodee appeared by his side.

"I'm good. I feel high as fuck though," Swerve noted.

"They gave you some Demerol after you came out of surgery."

"Surgery?" Swerve quizzed.

"Yeah, they had to do emergency surgery. The bullet hit one of the main arteries in your leg. You had to get some blood too because you lost a lot. You've been out all night," Rhapsodee explained.

"Damn," Swerve said before the door opened and the nurse walked in.

"Oh, you're awake. How are you?" she asked as she made her way to Swerve's bedside.

After she asked him a few more questions, the nurse left to go and get the doctor. It didn't take long for both of them to come back. Rhapsodee had been quiet ever since she told him what had happened while he was out of it.

"Mr. St. John. How are you feeling, young man?" the grey headed white man asked.

"I'm okay, I think. Feeling a little lightheaded and confused."

"Have you taken Demerol before?"

"No, never had pain meds besides Tylenol or Ibuprofen," Swerve confessed.

28

"One of the side effects is confusion and, in some cases, it can cause temporary amnesia. It's nothing to be alarmed about," the doctor confirmed.

He began doing the same thing that the nurse did, checking his vitals and asking different questions. A bright idea popped into Swerve's head and he forced himself not to let the smile show on his face.

"What exactly happened?"

"Your wife told us that she heard someone coming into the house and you were supposed to be at work, so she got scared and reacted quicker than she could think."

Swerve's face displayed total shock and confusion.

"It's okay. Don't worry about it right now baby," Rhapsodee chimed in.

"What happened though? How long do I have to stay here?"

"We'll keep an eye on you and you should be clear to go home first thing in the morning," the doctor confirmed.

"What's today?" Swerve inquired.

"It's Thursday baby," Rhapsodee replied.

Swerve closed his eyes and then grunted to let them know that he was frustrated. Rhapsodee continued to rub his hands, and he saw tears in her eyes when he looked at her. It appeared that his plan was working, and Swerve was happy with the shit. The doctor told Swerve to alert the nurse if he felt any pain and he nodded his head, letting him know that he would, but never opened his mouth. When the doctor and nurse left, Rhapsodee broke down and started crying.

"What are you crying for baby?" Swerve asked.

"Because it's my fault," she admitted.

"The reason I'm in here is your fault? How?" he asked.

"You don't remember anything that led up to this, Swerve?"

"My head hurts like fuck when I try to think back," Swerve said, closing his eyes.

"Don't worry about it right now. Just get some rest so you can get out of here."

29

Rhapsodee looked like she wanted to say more, but instead, she fluffed Swerve's pillow. He raised up and let her help him get comfortable. When she was done, he closed his eyes again. His plan was working. Swerve silently celebrated his victory and drifted off to sleep.

Chapter Seven

"Gotta hand it to you, you had me there for a while. I was so in love with you, I couldn't see past your smile. Now I smell the coffee, got a wake-up call, and it left a message that you just don't care at all." Leah sang along with Toni Braxton.

"Well damn," her friend Twin said from the passenger's seat.

"Giirrll, I felt that shit!" Leah exclaimed.

"Hell yeah, bitch. We can tell! Nigga got your nose wide open I see." Princess chimed in.

Twin and Princess bent over in laughter at Leah. She wasn't lying, she really felt that shit. It was time for her to get back to doing her. If E-Love didn't want to commit, that was fine but she damn sure wasn't about to be faithful to a nigga that wasn't hers. The three of them were on their way to Mobile, Alabama for some Mardi Gras festivities. It was crazy that as close as they were, last year was the first time that they ever attended. They had so much fun and Leah vowed to never miss it again. They planned on staying until Tuesday night so that they could be there for Fat Tuesday. Leah wanted Rhapsodee to go, but her cousin was stuck in her emotions, feeling guilty over shooting Swerve's crazy ass. Leah knew that her cousin had a heart of gold, so she didn't fault her. However, it seemed that she had too much heart for the nigga that she was with because he wasn't deserving of it.

The ride was smooth, and a few hours later, Leah turned into the parking lot of the Battle House Hotel in downtown Mobile. They checked in and went into their suite, thankful that the process wasn't long. By the time they made it to their room, got settled and took a few shots, it was damn near five o'clock. They planned on going to eat at Mudbugs before going out, so the trio gathered themselves and headed out.

Thirty minutes later, they pulled up and Leah's stomach began growling as soon as she smelled the food. Hands down, Mudbugs had some of the best damn seafood in the Mobile area and they weren't stingy with the shit either.

They made their way inside and the line was long as hell, but it moved fast. It wasn't a fancy restaurant or anything, but you were liable to see anybody there because of the food and great customer service. The smell of *Humme* by Dior filled Leah's nostrils. Searching for the source of the smell, she locked eyes with one of the most handsome men that she had ever seen. She could tell he was older by his style but definitely not by his looks, it wasn't often that Leah was at a loss for words, but she definitely was at that moment.

"You are the most stunning woman that I have ever seen in my life," the man said, grabbing Leah's hand and kissing it.

"Umm, yeah. Thank you," she replied after Princess nudged her.

"The name's Sebastian."

"I'm Delilah, but everyone calls me Leah."

"Leah, I like that. You're gonna be my sweet little Leah," he smiled, showing his pearly whites.

"What makes you think I'm gonna be anything?" She finally started acting like herself.

"I don't think, I know."

They talked as the line moved along, and when they made it to the front, Sebastian offered to pay for all of the girls meals. Leah tried to decline, but Sebastian nor her friends were having it. He got his food to go. Leah actually got a little sad because she was really enjoying his company and didn't want other little interactions to end. Her friends went and sat down while she walked outside with him. The Porsche that he was pushing looked like it had just rolled right off of the lot. It was just that damn clean. They talked for a few more minutes and then Leah reluctantly told him that she needed to get back to her friends. Sebastian didn't leave before getting her number and ending their encounter with a hug and a forehead kiss. Leah's panties got wet just at the touch and she wondered where the fuck Sebastian had been all of her life. She wanted to ask him his age, but honestly, it didn't even matter. He had shown interest in her and she was damn sure interested in him.

Hard and Ruthless

"Bitch, E-Love who? Somebody is about to let her inner thot out this weekend. Shit get that dick then," Sharon squealed once she made it back to where they were.

"This hooka done fell in love at first sight. That man is fine as hell and I can tell he was dripping in money," Twin chimed in.

"Y'all, I know right. I don't even know how to describe this feeling. This man is everything. Damn I almost ditched y'all asses for him," Leah said as she sat down and picked up one of her shrimps and peeled it.

"Hell, I don't blame you though. I wouldn't have even been mad," Princess expressed, and they all laughed.

"Y'all laughing, but I'm dead ass serious. Y'all know I live through y'all anyway," she continued.

They finished their food while talking shit to each other and then headed back to their hotel room for all of thirty minutes, changing clothes and heading back out. It was good that they were downtown because everything was within walking distance. Twin was the hardheaded one who wore heels, but she never complained, even though both Leah and Sharon knew those stilettos were kicking her ass after only an hour had passed. They ended up bar hopping and having hella fun until almost four o'clock the next morning. As soon as they made it back to the room, Leah passed out and didn't even bother wrapping her hair.

It was almost noon by the time they woke up. Leah noticed that she had a missed call from Sebastian. Butterflies formed in her stomach and she wondered what the fuck was wrong with her. She got up, washed her face, and brushed her teeth. Just when she was about to call Sebastian back, her phone rang with E-Love's picture appearing on the screen. She wanted to send his ass to voicemail but decided to go ahead and answer so that she could get him out of the way and get back to enjoying her weekend.

"Hello."

"Hey baby, come to room 358."

"Huh?" Leah was confused on why he said that.

"I just checked in. Come to room 358, unless you here with another nigga. What room y'all in?"

"You just checked in? The fuck? And don't play me like one of your little side bitches. Nigga it's just us. I'll be there in a minute, so chill out!" Leah hung up.

For the first time ever, Leah wished that she wasn't fucking with E-Love because she really was attracted to Sebastian. She knew that if she called him back, he was going to want to meet up and she couldn't plan anything until she figured out what all E-Love was planning on doing. She headed towards room 358, trying to figure out how to get rid of her partial boyfriend that didn't even claim her for the rest of the weekend.

Chapter Eight

"So, you think I'm a fake ass boss? That I fuck bitches more than I put in work? What else did he say Bobby B?" E-Love asked as he made circles around one of the workers that they had tied to a chair in the warehouse.

"Oh, he said you a pussy ass nigga too," Bobby B added.

"I knew I was missing something," E-Love shook his head in disbelief. "As good as I was to yo bitch ass, this the thanks I get? I was gone do some long drawn out torture type shit, but I ain't got the time. You ain't even worth it," E-Love said before he sent off a shot to his dome. "Tell them niggas to come clean this shit up," E-Love said to one of the youngsters on deck and walked out.

He purposely had them there, so they could see that he was still with the shits and didn't mind getting his hands dirty. It had been a minute since he had to off one of the niggas from the team, but no one was exempt. E-Love believed in treating everyone with love, but he wasn't naïve enough to think that niggas would forever be grateful. When he left the spot, E-Love made his way home to change clothes for a business meeting that he had and then he planned on hopping on 65 south heading to Mobile.

After a night of kicking it with the homies, E-Love and D'Lamar made their way to the hotel long after the sun had risen and handled a little business. He picked up his phone and called Leah while the blunt was in rotation, telling her to come to him.

E-Love could have easily stayed at his cousin's house while he was in Mobile, but he decided to cop a room where Leah was staying so that he could have some on demand pussy. He hadn't officially cut off any of his other hoes, but he had been ignoring calls and texts left and right for some reason that he didn't fully understand.

"Nigga let me go to my room before yo ol' in love ass put me out," D'Lamar joked.

"Fuck you, nigga. That's yo ass that be loving these hoes," E-Love fired back.

Once D'Lamar left, E-Love finished off the blunt that they had been sharing before cracking the door, leaving it open for Leah. It was a non-smoking hotel, but of course, money always talked. E-Love hopped in the shower and washed and rinsed off a couple of times. Once he stepped out of the shower, he dried off and then wrapped a towel around his waist. E-Love had kicked it all night and all morning, but he needed some pussy and a power nap before hitting the streets again. As soon as he finished brushing his teeth and walked out into the room, Leah was walking in.

"You didn't tell me you were coming here."

"Shiiiiiit, you ain't happy to see a nigga?"

"Of course, I am nigga. I just didn't know. You know I'm here with the girls," Leah walked over and laid on the bed.

"I know. I need some pussy though. I ain't tryin' to fuck with these lil thots you be accusing me of fuckin' wit," E-Love caught himself off guard by confessing.

He couldn't read the look that Leah was giving him, but he didn't waste much time trying to figure it out either. E-Love made his way to the bed, staring down at the beauty that was right in front of him. Before any other words could be spoken, he pressed his lips against hers and the shit took his breath away. Leah allowed his tongue to intertwine with hers and a few moments later, his towel fell to his feet, initiating E-Love's brick hard dick to stand at attention. Not knowing what had taken over him, E-Love decided to go with his feelings and kissed Leah from her lips to her neck. Once he went further down, he removed the tank top that she was wearing and went ahead and pulled her shorts off too, noticing that she didn't have any panties on. E-Love kissed her from head to toe and her moans only made his dick harder. He made her cum twice with his tongue alone and then finally slid into her wetness. E-Love made sweet love to Leah for the next forty-five minutes and the shit was amazing. He was ready to fire up his blunt as soon as he nutted inside of her, collapsing right beside her.

"Damn, what got into you? You ain't never did that shit before. You must have been really missing this pussy." Leah questioned after a few minutes of them lying beside each other.

"Hell, if I know, but that shit was good. I won that whole round though," he smirked.

"Nigga shut up," she playfully hit him.

E-Love's mind was all over the place. He wanted to say so much but didn't know how to form the gotdam words. He said fuck it and rolled over, getting ready to let it out. However, Leah's phone rang and he glimpsed at the name "Sebastian" popping up on the screen. His words got caught in his throat.

"What in the fuck? What kind of shit you trying to pull, bitch? Who the fuck is that? Answer me now dammit!" He became instantly pissed off, jumping up from the bed.

Von Wiley Hall

Chapter Nine

It had almost been a week since Rhapsodee shot Swerve. She had taken time off of work catering to his every need. To say she felt bad about what she did was an understatement. On top of Swerve's memory loss, he had to go to therapy so he could bounce back quicker and Rhapsodee was right by his side. She really wanted to bring up their marital issues, but guilt consumed her every time she got ready to say something. There was a constant reminder of what she had done, therefore she couldn't bring herself to speak on it. She watched Swerve do his leg exercises and noticed that he was on his last set. She gathered her things and slowly made her way towards him.

"You did great honey," Rhapsodee said as they exited through the door.

"Yeah?" he asked with astonishment lacing his voice.

"Of course, don't you feel a little better?"

"I guess I do. I'll be glad when I know everything again. I get headaches trying to figure shit out," Swerve admitted.

Rhapsodee pondered on how she was going to address her work situation.

She received an email for a job in Texas that would last a couple of weeks, and it was going to pay her sixty dollars an hour plus travel. The only thing stopping her was that she had to reply with an answer within the next couple of hours and leave the next morning. She helped Swerve get situated in the passenger's seat, got in herself, and then drove off.

"What you want to eat?" Rhapsodee queried, hoping that he didn't ask for a home cooked meal because she really didn't want to cook.

"We can just grab something from somewhere since you been cooking every day. How about we order something from American Deli?"

"Sounds good to me. Go ahead and place the order and I can head that way."

"Cool, I'm on it now."

She listened as Swerve placed the order for their favorite wings. Once he was done, Rhap decided to go ahead and get her dilemma out of the way.

"I got an email about a new assignment this morning. I didn't reply yet because I wanted to talk to you."

"Where is it?" he asked.

"Texas. I'm not sure how long yet," Rhap lied before he asked.

Even though she was basically kissing his ass, she wasn't about to be a fool anymore.

"Well you've been taking care of me and you said yourself, I'm bouncing back quick, so I know it's time for you to get back to work. I understand baby. I'm gon' hate for you to leave, but I understand," Swerve expressed.

"Are you sure? I'll have to leave in the morning for this particular job, but I can't get Leah to come over and..."

"No, no, baby/ I'm good. It's time for us to get back on track anyway. I'm gonna call Raymond about a construction job he has his hands in and try to line something up too. It's time for me to get back to spoiling you."

Rhapsodee smiled, relieved that the conversation had gone so well. She really felt like Swerve would be okay. Plus, she really didn't want to pass up on that job, so she was elated that she could go home and pack. Even though he didn't want Leah checking up on him, Rhap still tossed the idea around in her head about asking her cousin to slide through every now and then. She knew Leah couldn't stand his ass, but on the strength of her, she would do whatever. About thirty minutes later, she turned into American Deli, and Swerve insisted on going inside to get the food. While she waited for him to return, Rhap pulled her phone out and scrolled through Instagram liking pictures. A picture of her cousin and friends from Mardi Gras popped and Rhap got a little sad that she had to back out. Right after she double hearted the picture, her phone rang, and she answered.

"Bitch, I was just looking at the pictures you posted. I'm so jealous."

"Yo ass coulda left that loser at home and joined us," Leah replied. "But listen, I think I'm in love!!" Leah sang.

"Leah, you weren't fooling nobody but yourself. You been in love with E-Love," Rhap rolled her eyes.

"Shut up and listen girl. I met this older guy and nigga made me forget my own name for a minute," Leah confessed.

"Wait, wait. What? This must be somebody with some bomb ass dick. I never heard you sound like this before."

"I didn't even sleep with him yet, heifer. Oh, but I can't wait!' Leah exclaimed.

"Damnnn. My cousin all sprung and ain't even gave it up yet. This is definitely a first."

"I know right!" Leah laughed and couldn't help but to agree.

"So, what's this man's name and what are you gonna do about E-Love since you've fallen in love at first sight?"

"His name is Sebastian, and E-Love's playing games anyway."

"Umm, you still love him so you ain't fooling me. Damn, here comes Swerve. We gon' have to continue this conversation tomorrow when I land."

"Oh, you're going back to work? Good! Tell that loser he needs to be doing the same thing."

"Bye Leah," Rhapsodee hung up before her cousin could reply. She knew that Leah would go on and on and on.

"That was fast," Rhap said once Swerve got back in and got settled."

"Yeah, I thought the wait was gon' be a lil longer too, but we good to go."

Rhapsodee put the car in gear and headed home. Traffic was heavy, so it took almost thirty minutes for what should have been a ten-minute drive. They made it home, ate their wings together, and then Rhap ran a nice hot bubble bath for herself. As soon as she undressed and stepped inside, she sank into the hot water. With her eyes closed, Rhap commanded Siri to play her slow jams playlist and the first song that played was her wedding song. A tear slid down Rhap's left cheek before she was able to stop it. After the one tear fell, she couldn't stop the rest of them and suddenly, she felt her tears being wiped away.

"What's wrong babe?" Swerve asked as he continued to rub her cheeks.

"I just miss the way things were," she finally admitted.

"What changed?" he quizzed, still playing the amnesia role perfectly.

Rhapsody had temporarily forgotten about Swerve's temporary memory loss. She was silently thankful that she was leaving the next day because she didn't know how much more she would be able to take.

"A lot happened that you don't remember right now. I think we should go to counseling," she confessed.

"Counseling? You think we need counseling?"

"Yes baby, I do."

"Well, I'm willing to do whatever it takes to make our marriage work," Swerve agreed, shocking the shit out of Rhapsodee.

Swerve sat on the edge of the tub and began massaging her shoulders. His touch felt good as hell, and moans escaped her lips when he began teasing her nipples. It had been a little over three weeks since Rhap had some and she was really needing a fix. Flashbacks of what she came home from work to popped into her head once again, but she quickly pushed them out. Since she was leaving the next morning, she needed to get some so she would be good. When she got out of the tub, she allowed her husband to have his way.

Chapter Ten

Swerve kissed his wife goodbye and assured her for the hundredth time that he would be okay. It was six minutes after five when he laid back down to catch some more z's. When he woke back up and grabbed his phone, he had a text message from Rhapsodee, letting him know that her flight was leaving. He didn't even hear his phone. He glanced at the time and saw that it was almost nine o'clock. After taking a piss, washing his face, and brushing his teeth, Swerve went to the kitchen and made himself a bowl of Raisin Bran. He sat there eating his cereal, feeling like Morris Chestnut. He was so happy that Rhapsodee was gone back to work and was even happier that his acting had paid off. Swerve didn't know how much longer he would be able to keep up his façade without his wife seeing through it. His wife was smart, but he knew she was acting off of guilt and emotions at the moment. A text came through and Swerve picked up his phone, sighing after he read it.

Yoshi: We need to talk TODAY!! And I'm not taking no for an answer so don't fuckin play wit me. I'll text you the address on where you need to meet me. Get ready now!

Swerve blew out a frustrated breath and then rubbed his temples. He knew that Yoshi would pop back up sooner or later. She had been way too quiet, and he knew how she operated. For that reason alone, he finished up with his cereal and then went to get his day started. Swerve went into the master bathroom and turned on the shower. After the water warmed up, he stepped inside and took a quick shower. Not knowing what Yoshi had up her sleeve, Swerve moved in a hurry so that he could be ready for whatever. When he stepped out of the shower, he dried off, put on lotion, and then threw on a black and red Polo jogger and a pair of J's.

As soon as he finished lacing his shoes, his phone rang, and he knew that it was Rhap by the ring tone.

"Hey baby, you had a safe flight?"

"I did, just hopped in the Uber and headed to my room. What are you up to? How are you feeling?"

"I just finished eating some cereal, 'bout to hop on the computer now and look up some jobs. I'm feeling fine though. I miss you."

"I miss you too. I just wanted to let you know I made it. I'll let you know when I get settled."

"Alright boo. I love you!"

"I love you too!"

Swerve was glad the Rhap called before he left home, and he was more thankful that she didn't FaceTime. He was more than sure that the next call would be a FaceTime call so he hoped that Yoshi would hit him up so that he could handle whatever bullshit she was on. As soon as he made it to the living room, Yoshi texted him an address, and he grabbed his keys and headed out of the door. Once he got comfortable in his car, Swerve tapped on the address and opened it in maps. Siri alerted him that the drive was thirty-two minutes away. He was glad that he decided to go to therapy because he didn't even need the crutches anymore. When he walked, he limped a little bit, but it wasn't anything too major.

Swerve had been following the directions without paying any attention to his surroundings. He was confused as fuck when he pulled up to a clinic, wondering what kinda games Yoshi's ass was on that time around. He grabbed his phone after he parked and called her.

"Come inside," she said and hung right up before he had a chance to respond.

"This girl gon' make me choke her ass out," Swerve mumbled as he made his way inside.

Yoshi was sitting in a chair by the window and filling out paperwork on a clipboard when he walked in. A little boy was sitting to the right of her, so he bypassed and sat on the other side.

"Yoshi, what you got me at the clinic with you for? Don't tell me you done burned me?" Swerve whispered.

"Nigga you got me fucked up. If anybody burned anybody, you know damn well you would be the one doing the burning," she spat.

The girl beside them laughed but looked away when Swerve made eye contact with her.

"So, what we doin' here, man? I ain't got time for no bullshit."

"Oh, this ain't no bullshit. I went through my first pregnancy without you, you gone be here every step of the way for this one," Yoshi coolly replied.

"What you mean first pregnancy? And you pregnant now?"

Instead of Yoshi replying, she got up and walked to the window, handing them the clipboard. She stood there talking for a few minutes and Swerve finally took the time to look at the little boy. He was sitting there with headphones in, playing a video game. If he had to guess, he would say that the boy was about four years old, and Swerve wondered why he wasn't in school. The striking resemblance that the boy had to him was crazy as fuck. Swerve had a feeling that his world was about to really be shook up. Not that it already wasn't, but with his memory loss, he was able to forget about reality.

"James Jr., remember I told you that you get to meet someone special today?" Yoshi said as she removed the headphones from her son's ears, and he nodded his head yes.

"Well here's your daddy. Swerve, meet your son, J.J."

Swerve broke out into a coughing fit right after Yoshi had just confirmed what he had been thinking.

"Son? Yoshi, what the hell? You've had a son this whole time and didn't say shit? How I know he…"

"Say that shit out loud and I'll cut yo dick off. Don't insult me James St. John!" Yoshi fumed.

Swerve head began spinning. He was already in deep shit, and it just kept getting deeper. He knew Yoshi was a good girl. She was just stuck on his ass. He couldn't lie, though. He loved her, but he loved Rhapsodee and his ass loved other bitches from time to time as well.

"Hi," J.J. spoke and broke Swerve out of his thoughts.

"Hey there lil buddy. How are you?"

"I'm fine. It's great to meet you, but where have you been?" J.J. asked, shocking the hell out of Swerve.

"I, ummm, well honestly, I didn't know anything about you," Swerve stuttered.

"Baby, remember how we just moved from Kentucky to here? Mommy met your daddy years ago and he lived here in this state. Now, we'll be closer, and he can spend time with you," Yoshi explained, causing Swerve to bite his tongue to keep from cussing her ass out.

"Yoshi Brevardo!" a nurse called out.

"Come on sweetie, let's go and see what mommy is having. Come on dad," Yoshi addressed J.J. and then Swerve.

Swerve reluctantly got up from his chair, and as soon as he did, his cell phone rang with a FaceTime call from Rhapsodee. There was no way that he could answer that call at the women's clinic. He sighed and knew that his temporary memory loss wasn't about to get him out of the bullshit that he had just sank into.

Chapter Eleven

Yoshi walked towards the back with J.J. following her, and if Swerve knew what was good for him, he would be following closely behind as well. She loved Swerve's dirty drawers, but she told herself that he had shit on her for the last muthafuckin' time. Once Yoshi did some hardcore investigating and found out the details about why Swerve abandoned her years ago, her heart was broken into pieces. She never even told him she had a son, but when she took about ten home pregnancy tests a few months ago, she decided that she was going to make Swerve man up and take care of his responsibilities. She didn't fault Rhapsodee, but it was time for Swerve to play by her rules.

"Step right in here so we can get your weight and blood pressure. The rest of your family can go right to that waiting area," the nurse nicely stated.

Yoshi smiled at her words and ignored the stares she felt coming from Swerve. She stepped onto the scale and then got her blood pressure checked.

"Your blood pressure is 168/96. That's in the prehypertension range. Do you take meds?"

"No, I just been a little stressed lately, but everything is finally looking up now," Yoshi smiled as she thought about how her stress would really be gone once the rest of her plans came into action.

"Okay, I'll check it again before you leave, but for now, we need a urine sample. The bathroom is right across the hall. Place the sample in the window once you're done."

Yoshi took the cup and did as she was instructed. A few minutes later, she took a seat beside Swerve and J.J.

"Yoshi, you know this is fucked up, right?" Swerve whispered.

"Let's not get started on what's fucked up sweetheart. My first mind was to cut your dick off and make you suck it, so I suggest you shut the fuck up and go along with plan b!"

The look on Swerve's face gave Yoshi the satisfaction that she needed for the moment. She had only shown her crazy side to him once, so he knew it was real, but she prayed that she wouldn't have to go down that road again. Yoshi looked over at her son and was happy that he was tuned into his game and oblivious to what was going on. A few minutes later, her name was called, and she followed the nurse to an examination room. She was asked a hundred questions and then her pregnancy was confirmed.

"According to your last period, you appear to be about fourteen weeks, but we'll do an ultrasound and confirm everything. Lay back for me."

As soon as Yoshi laid back, she noticed Swerve was looking at his phone once again. Judging by his demeanor, she knew that it had to be Rhapsodee calling.

"Baby, this is a happy time for us. Turn the phone off."

Moments later, a heartbeat could be heard, and Yoshi's smile spread a mile wide.

"Is that my brother?" J.J. stood up beside his mom and asked.

"Well we don't know if you'll have a brother or sister yet baby."

"I want a brother," J.J. announced.

"Well little fella, your mommy is almost to the point where we will be able to tell. You'll know in a few weeks," the nurse smiled and J.J. returned the smile.

"So, what's my due date?" Yoshi inquired.

A few minutes later, the doctor walked in and pretty much summed up everything that had already been said. Yoshi was informed to stop by the front desk to schedule her next appointment. Once that was done, she made her way outside and instructed J.J. to get in the car and wait. She knew that Swerve was ready to explode at any moment, and it was time to lay the ground rules.

"Yoshi, what the fuck man? You done lost yo gotdam mind?" Swerve based as soon as they were alone.

"Not yet, but I am if you think you gon' keep fuckin' playin' me. I've been nothing but good to yo trifling ass and enough is enough. I'm not dealing with yo bullshit no more. We moved to an apartment out in Lithonia. That's a safe enough distance from you for the time being. I'm gonna give you a little time to get yo shit together, but once this baby is born, WE gon' be a family. For now, you better figure out how to bounce back and forth. This single parent shit is for the birds. Grow the fuck up and stop playing games!" Yoshi spat and left Swerve standing there with a stupid ass look on his face.

Von Wiley Hall

Chapter Twelve

Leah left work Friday, ready for the weekend. She was excited as hell, and it was getting harder and harder to contain it. Not that she wanted to or had to, but she had a lie ready for E-Love because she planned on being missing in action. To her surprise, he made things easier for her when he called and said that he had to make a run and would be gone for a couple of days. Leah left work on cloud nine. The first stop she was making was to the nail shop. Her hair was still in braids that her cousin Stacey did for her, so she decided that she would either pin them up or let them hang. About thirty minutes later, Leah pulled up to the nail shop and parked.

Since it was early in the day, she was in and out in an hour with both a manicure and a pedicure. Leah went through the drive thru at Popeye's and grabbed a chicken meal with a strawberry soda and then headed home to grab her bag, so she could hit the road. She could have easily hopped on the highway after leaving the nail shop, but her cousin begged her to take Swerve something to eat. Even though she didn't give a shit about him, she loved her cousin and would always help her out in any way that she could. When Leah pulled up at home, she was pretty much done with her food and thought about letting Swerve's get colder, but she headed to their building and knocked on the door.

"Who is it?" he asked after a few minutes.

"Boy, open this damn door. I know Rhap texted yo ass!"

"Leah, yo ass gon' stop being so rude." The locks clicked, and the door finally opened.

Leah shoved the bag in Swerve's hands and then brushed past him. She heard him talking, but she ignored his ass and searched the apartment, making sure he didn't have another bitch in there, again. Once Leah was satisfied, she left without saying another word and left the door wide open. He couldn't limp his ass back and close it. Rhap had actually asked Leah to check on Swerve before, but then she called and changed her mind, saying that he had been doped up on his meds and was sleeping a lot. Leah was willing to bet that the nigga was up to no good, but he wasn't her problem.

About thirty minutes later, Leah was cruising down 285 E, singing along with Ella Mai, smiling as she headed to her weekend getaway. Sebastian told her that he wanted to spend some time with her, and she hurriedly agreed and couldn't wait. The ringing of her phone interrupted the music and Leah saw that it was her girl calling and slid the bar to answer.

"Hey girl!"

"What up trick? You on the road?" Twin inquired.

"Yes, I'm so excited. Girl, I still can't figure out what it is about this man, but I'm so drawn to him," Leah bubbled.

"Hell, I can. Now you know we all seen that print!"

"Shut uppp! I can't stand you!" Leah was crying laughing.

"You know I'm right. But for real though, I can hear it in your voice. Well you know I'll be waiting on all the juicy details since I'm living through you. What you tell E-Love?"

"Oh, girl he's outta town on business, so I'm good to go. Not that he's my man anyways. He's doing him and I'm definitely about to do me," Leah rolled her eyes.

"Shit, I hear ya talkin'. Do you then, trick. Look at it this way, this might be what it takes for him to get right. Someone else having your attention. E-Love wanna do what he wanna do, but you supposed to be faithful. That's that crazy shit I don't like. But you know how men are. When the first one won't the next one will," Twin explained.

"Girl, you might be right. But lemme ask you this, you think I'ma hoe?" Leah pondered.

"Now trick, if you didn't think you were a hoe getting with four guys over a weekend period years ago, then your ass definitely not a hoe now!" Twin reminded Leah of a wild and crazy weekend sexcapade she had years ago.

Leah couldn't help but laugh. "Twin, I can't stand you," she chuckled. "You didn't have to go there, but man that was a great weekend." She couldn't help but to reminisce about the shit she pulled back then. Her kitty was sore, but definitely satisfied that weekend.

They talked for about an hour. The conversation consisted of every damn thing, just like always. When Leah finally hung up, her music started blasting again and she picked up right where she left off. The miles got on down and shortly after five o'clock, Leah was turning into the parking lot of the Marriott that was right across the street from Red Lobster. Sebastian had tickets to the Atlanta Braves game, and he made it known that he had a full weekend planned for the two of them. Even though Leah was more than ready to break Sebastian off with some sex, she decided to book her own room and meet up with him in a couple of hours.

About an hour and a few drinks later, Leah's phone rang, and butterflies fluttered her stomach when she saw the name that she had saved for Sebastian.

"Are you ready, beautiful?" his sexy voice spoke as soon as she answered the phone.

"I am. You ready for me to head down now?" she cooed.

"I'm in the lobby."

The call ended and Leah slipped into her blue, red, and white air max. She had changed clothes three times, but finally decided on something comfortable since it was a game that they were going to. Leah made her way to the lobby and the scent of Sebastian's cologne hit her nostrils before she even saw him. Once she laid eyes on him, she saw that he was dressed down in an expensive Atlanta Braves jersey and she was glad that she took the dress and heels off.

Sebastian made his way to her, lifted her hand, and kissed it as soon as he was within reach, making her panties wet.

Damn I gotta get myself together, Leah thought to herself.

The duo walked hand in hand outside and Sebastian led her to a black Suburban and opened the back door.

"We're not gonna walk over?"

"Of course not. It seems close, but that's actually a good little walk, and I don't want you getting all tired on me," he winked and got in right behind here.

As the driver made his way to Phipps Center, Leah noticed that it really was further away than it appeared, and she was happy that Sebastian had it all figured out. They got dropped off as close as possible and the line was long as hell already. Sebastian bypassed the line and Leah held onto his hand and followed him. They made it to the elevator where Sebastian flashed something that gained them access. That same process was done a couple of more times and they ended up top where the suites were located. She knew that he was well connected when they first met, she reconfirmed that he was really the man when they entered Platinum Club.

"We have courtside seats, if you wanna go down at any time, but I figured we would kick it here first. Help yourself to anything," Sebastian entreated.

Leah ended up meeting a few of Sebastian's friends and their women, and she could tell right off that they felt like she was too young for him. She played the nice role for as long as she could before finally taking Sebastian up on the courtside seats offer right before halftime. As soon as they sat in their seats, the kiss cam game was going on and landed right on them.

Sebastian caught her off guard with their kiss and the shit had her ready to leave the game right then and there.

Chapter Thirteen

E-Love was cruising on Interstate 20 headed east to meet up with one of his partners in Birmingham. His right-hand man, Bobby B, was in the passenger's seat rolling up. E-Love didn't make it a habit of riding dirty, but his stress level had been high as fuck lately. He found himself drinking and smoking more than normal. As much as he hated to admit it, Leah's nonchalant attitude and behavior was fuckin' with him. Street shit had been going on too, and E-Love caught a couple of bodies earlier that week, but that was normal.

"This shit actually aight," Bobby B verbalized and then lit the backwood.

"Yeah it is," E-Love agreed.

Bobby B passed the backwood and E-Love took two deep pulls. He was about to take another one until his homie stopped him.

"Damn nigga. Puff, puff, pass," Bobby B joked.

"Shit, my bad man."

"What's been up with you? Besides the business shit, yo ass been seeming distracted," Bobby B probed.

"Man, to be honest, I really can't even explain the shit. You ever thought about settling down and shit?" E-Love questioned his boy.

"Settling downnnn? Nigga hell naw! For what?"

"See I knew I couldn't talk to yo ass about shit," E-Love laughed, taking the blunt back and hitting it again.

"I'm just being honest, but I ain't you and I don't have a down ass chick like Leah. If I did, I wouldn't even be on these hoes like that. Leah is smart, a down ass chick, she works, and not to mention, she fine as fuck," Bobby B explained.

"Hold up nigga. I get it but damn," E-Love cut him off.

"I'm just saying, let me find a Leah and watch what I do. I can't believe she done put up with yo shit for this long. You better lock her ass down before she gets away."

E-Love knew that Bobby B was speaking from experience. He used to always vent about the real one that he let get away. Instead of opening up to love again, Bobby B entertained all types of females with no strings attached. That was exactly what E-Love had been doing as well, but the connection that he had with Leah was fucking with him. Normally, he wouldn't give a damn if females he fucked had other niggas, but not Leah. Music and good conversation made the trip fly by and E-Love was pulling up to the hotel in no time. Him and Bobby B went and checked into their rooms, and E-Love sent a text to his homie, letting him know that everything was on schedule.

Since they planned on hitting up the club right after the meeting, E-Love laid his clothes out on the bed in preparation to take a shower. He grabbed his phone and scrolled to Leah's name, but threw the phone down instead of dialing her number like he wanted to. The fact that she hadn't called or texted him was a shock, but he would deal with her ass after taking care of business. Thirty minutes later, E-Love was headed to the lobby to meet up with Bobby B. It was a quarter till eight and their meeting was ser for nine thirty. The spot was about twenty minutes away, so they had plenty of time. The guys were planning to hang out at Onyx afterwards, and E-Love was ready to throw back a couple of shots.

They pulled up to the spot and both E-Love and Bobby B checked their surroundings out of instinct. He saw a white Escalade pulling up and knew that it had to be his boy. One of the reasons they had been successful with staying out of jail was because of how they all moved and switched up locations for handling business. E-Love got out and Bobby B was right on his heels.

"What up bruh? You and Bobby B already met, so we can get right down to business. You met this nigga before today?" E-Love quizzed.

"Nah fam, but I'm ready and I know y'all are too. I hope ain't no fuck shit goin' on."

"Let's see what it is then," Bobby B chimed in and they made their way to the door.

The three of them made their way inside and were surprised that no security was in sight. To E-Love, that put him on high alert. Before he could say anything, the man that they were meeting appeared. E-Love knew it was him because of the research he had done.

"Welcome fellas. Let's get right down to business," the guy motioned for them to have a seat.

Each of them took their time, but they finally sat down and got right on down to business. E-Love couldn't believe that the price of the product was so low. The shit seemed too good to be true. He could tell that both of his boys felt the same way from the change in their body language that he could see through his peripheral vision.

"How are you able to offer these prices?" E-Love quizzed when there was a moment of silence.

"Let's just say I made the right connections and I'm able to take the risk."

"A'ight. Well we'll think about it and get back with ya," E-Love advised.

His homie started getting up and Bobby B followed suit. They had been in crazy situations before and knew the drill. E-Love had a weird feeling and prayed he was wrong, but he was prepared for whatever.

"The offer expires in twenty-four hours," the guy called out to them.

"We gotta get the fuck away from here," E-Love said as soon as they made it outside.

"I agr..."

Pop!
Pop!
Pop!
Pop!
Pop!
Pht!
Pht!
Pht!
Pht!

"Let's get outta here now, y'all!" E-Love fumed. Me and Bobby B hopped into the car at the same time.

"Them niggas did a drive by with the regular pistols. Amateurs. We gotta get them fuck boys," Bobby B based, and E-Love agreed.

A text came through from his boy with a meeting spot and E-Love replied back confirming it. He had the sudden urge to just hear Leah's voice. She didn't know it, but she was actually his peace, so he put his pride to the side and dialed her number, only for her not to pick up.

Chapter Fourteen

Rhapsodee pulled into her parking lot and let out a deep breath. She loved her job, but it was always good to be home. She saw Swerve's car in his spot. Normally, she would get butterflies in her stomach at just the thought of him, but those feelings seemed to have faced overnight after catching him with his dick down another woman's throat. The two-week work assignment flew by, but during that time, Rhapsodee had a lot of time to think. She had also done a little research on the medicine that Swerve had been given. There was no cut and dry answer, but in most cases, the temporary amnesia should have worn off within a week. Rhapsodee thought about confronting Swerve right away, but the more she thought about it, letting him hang himself would work so much better. Right before Rhapsodee got out of the car, her phone rang. She smiled when she saw that it was her mom calling.

"Hey mom. How are you?"

"Well, now that I know you're alive and well, I'm fine. You never called me back and I've called you a few times."

"I'm sorry mom. I've had a lot going on and then I left for work and I'm just now getting back," Rhap explained.

"What's wrong with my baby? Is it that no good Swerve?" Jonetta asked.

Rhapsodee thought long and hard about whether she should tell her mom what was going on with Swerve or not. It was no secret that Jonetta didn't like Swerve, but the good thing about it, they didn't have to see each other often. Rhapsodee decided to give her mom a snippet of her concerns, leaving out all of the cheating details. Her mom gave her undivided attention and listened attentively just like she always did.

"Are you sure you're telling me everything?" her mom wondered after she was done talking.

"Yes mom. I don't want you worried. Married couples have issues, right? Everything will be fine," Rhap vacillated.

"If you say so darling, but it sounds like you're trying to convince yourself more than me," Jonetta beseeched.

"I love you mom and I'll talk to you later."

"I love you too baby."

After hanging up with her mom, Rhap got her bags out and made her way to her condo. She hadn't called Swerve to let him know that she was headed home. Rhap said a silent prayer that shit wouldn't backfire again as she put her key into the lock and twisted it. When she opened the door, the scent of a Febreze plug-in hit her in the face, and she knew that Swerve had been doing his spring cleaning. She made her way inside with hopes that he was back to his old self so that they could have a real conversation and move forward.

"Hey baby," Rhap found Swerve in the kitchen and walked over and gave him a kiss.

"Hey love. I had a feeling you would be here soon," he squeezed her ass.

"Yeah. I wanted to surprise you," she said and peeked into the pots that were on the stove.

"We in sync, girl. You forgot how we used to feel each other?" Swerve tested her.

"I guess I did," Rhap smiled.

"If you remember that, that means that you're back to normal huh?" she continued.

"I'm not sure. I still don't remember why you shot me, but I'm sure I'll be back one hundred soon. I had an interview yesterday and I should be receiving a call soon."

"That's great baby. I'm so happy for you. I think getting back into a routine will help you out so much. Is this the hookup from Raymond?" Rhap ignored her gut feeling and focused on the positive.

"Yep, and he wants to celebrate tomorrow night, but if you have plans, I can cancel on him."

"No, no, that's fine. Leah wants to have a girl's night in. I told her I would get back with her after I talked to you, so looks like we both can kick it with our friends," Rhap explained.

"As long as you good wit it. It's all about you ma," Swerve wrapped his arms around her body and squeezed her ass.

Hard and Ruthless

They shared a kiss, but surprisingly, Rhap felt nothing. She knew that he was in need of some sex and so was she, so she did something that she had never done before. She visualized another man and then made love to her husband.

Von Wiley Hall

Chapter Fifteen

Rhapsodee pulled up to the Hilton out in Sandy Springs and parked on the side. Instead of gathering at one of their places, the girls decided to get a room so that they could kick back and relax. It had been a minute since they had a slumber party and Rhap fought for a night instead of going out and clubbing. She went inside and checked into the suite. As soon as she made it to the fourth floor, Leah sent a text saying she was about to pull in. Surprisingly, Leah didn't even put up a fuss to go out. Honestly, Rhap was still shocked as hell because everyone knew that her cousin was the life of the party.

Thirty minutes later, Rhap, Leah, Princess, Sharon and Twin were throwing back shots, stuffing their faces with pizza and wings, listening to music and talking plenty of shit.

"Y'all, I think Swerve is lying about his memory loss, but I'm tryna let him hang himself since I can't really prove it," Rhap confessed, finally breaking the ice and getting down to the good stuff.

"You want me to beat that niggas ass? Just say the word and we can go right now! You know I'm down for whatever," Leah jumped up but then fell right back down onto the bed.

"Calm down trick, with ya drunk ass. Your ass can't even walk right now, but talking' about whoopin' ass," Twin chimed in, causing everyone to laugh.

"Let me make everyone a fresh drink," Sharon got up and went to the bar.

"Girl how and why did you take off on a Friday night?" Rhap asked Sharon.

"Needed a break. Now why you think he's lying?"

"Let's just call it women's intuition," Rhap replied and devoured another wing.

"I think you should let it play out like you're thinking. And I also think you should do everything possible to make your marriage work. This is what you've always wanted," says Princess.

"Princess, please don't start with that bullshit. Now I do agree Rhap should do what she wants, but don't try to act like Swerve forgot to pay the light bill or some shit. That nigga got caught with his dick down another woman's throat. In their home at that!" Twin fumed, getting heated just thinking about the disrespectful shit Swerve pulled.

"Wait, wait, wait, what?" Sharon quizzed.

"Oh, my bad. I've been too busy to fill you in," Rhap sighed.

"Nah you didn't tell her because you didn't feel comfortable enough to tell her ass. Why is she here anyway?" Leah chided.

"Leah, what did I ever do to you?"

"Yeah, Leah. Chill out. We're all here to kick back and have a good time. Now let's talk about this mystery man of yours," Rhap pleaded to her cousin with her eyes.

It was true that she didn't know Sharon all that well, but Rhapsodee felt sorry for her because she had recently lost her parents due to gun violence in Boston and decided that she was over the city and moved south. Rhap just wanted to be a friend to her so that she wouldn't be lonely, but that didn't stop Leah from talking shit.

"Yeah Leah, tell us about Mr. Irresistible," Twin cackled, saying that latter in a sing-song voice.

"Doesn't the name say it all?" Leah beamed, trying to twerk her little ass, but fell her drunk ass back on the bed.

Rhap smiled from ear to ear. Deep down, she knew that her cousin wanted to be E-Love, but it wouldn't hurt to entertain someone else to put some fire under his ass. Rhapsodee always admired her cousin for doing whatever she wanted. If she was that bold, she would leave Swerve and have some fun of her own, but she couldn't make herself do it. In her mind, she wanted to do just what Princess suggested, and if it just so happened to not work, her conscience would be clear.

"I'm happy for you trick, but you know E-Love gon' beat yo ass then beat up the kitty," Twin said, and the girls burst out laughing again.

"Speaking of E-Love, that nigga is a cock blocker, and he don't even know it. Why every single time me and my bae was about to take it there, his ass called?" Leah rolled her eyes.

"Wait, you still ain't gave him none yet?" Rhap queried.

"Nooo, I'm telling y'all. I wanted to so bad, but every time E-Love called, I just froze up," Leah admitted.

"Well it sounds like you got two good men, so you need to decide which one you want before I decide for you," Sharon challenged.

"What the fuck! What you say bitch?" Leah jumped up.

"Wait, wait," Rhap hopped up and stepped in between them.

"Chill Leah. It's girl's night and I'm just talking shit like everybody else."

"Ummm no the hell you not. We ain't talking shit like you, but you got us fucked up. You don't know us like that, but you're definitely about to find out. Play with it if you want to," Twin and Princess spoke.

The two of them hopped up, holding Leah back because Sharon's comment had really struck a nerve.

"Rhap you better tell your lil friend I don't play that shit! Commenting on shit that ain't her fucking business gonna fuck around and get more than her feelings hurt," Leah spat.

"Oh, my gawd. Come on y'all, this is supposed to be our fun night," Rhap pleaded.

"Today was a rough day for me, and I just wanted to have some fun, but I'll leave. I'm not wanted here anyway," Sharon sobbed and started gathering her things.

"Wait, Sharon. You don't have to leave," Rhap said.

"Yes, the fuck she does Rhapsodee! I know how you feel about her so you can go and comfort her, but she's not staying here with us," Leah commanded.

Rhap was stuck between a rock and a hard place. She was excited about the sleepover, but she knew that Leah already didn't care for Sharon and there was no making amends. She would feel like shit if she let Sharon leave alone, so she sucked it up, told the other girls goodnight, and decided to invite Sharon to her place. She has some liquor there, so they could finish the night, and she could also tell Sharon about herself in a sisterly way without the other girls.

"So much for the night of fun I had planned," Rhap sighed as she left the hotel with Sharon in tow.

Von Wiley Hall

Chapter Sixteen

"Y'all having an all-night thing or what?" Swerve asked his wife while he was getting dressed.

"Hmmm, I'm not sure really. I guess it just depends on how everything goes," she replied.

"Aight, well I'll be home around midnight or so. We just gon' drink and shoot some pool," he expressed.

"Sounds good babe."

Rhap gave him a kiss and then left. Swerve looked at the time and noticed that it was almost eight. He mentally mapped his night out and hurried up and finished getting dressed. He locked up and called Raymond as soon as he got in the car.

"What up bruh? You wanna shoot some pool and drink?" Swerve invited him after Raymond answered the phone.

"Nigga, you know I told you I was going outta town with my girl today."

"Oh yeah, I forgot. Aight then nigga," Swerve replied and hung up after talking to Raymond for a few more minutes about the job.

Swerve continued driving and forty-five minutes later, he pulled up to his destination. He grabbed his phone and sent a text telling Yoshi to come outside. She instantly replied, telling him to come inside. They were supposed to be going out to eat, but Swerve secretly hoped that she had changed her mind and decided to stay in. That would help him out tremendously. He made his way to the door, pulled out his key, inserted it, and gained entrance to his home away from home. The aroma of whatever Yoshi was cooking filled his nostrils and instantly caused his stomach to growl.

"Heeey baby," Yoshi cooed as she walked up to him and gave him a kiss. "I decided to cook for you. We can just chill here. J.J. is in there playing the game, so you can go and join him while I finish up."

That was music to Swerve's ears. For the past two weeks, he had been the family man to Yoshi and J.J. He answered Rhap's FaceTime calls while he was in the bathroom with only his face showing or in the bed late at night with the lights out. Most times, he blamed his pain meds on putting him to sleep. Shit had been smooth so far, but Swerve knew that he was going to catch hell while Rhapsodee was home. Her girl's night worked out perfectly, giving him a few free hours without any worries. The only thing he hoped was that Yoshi didn't trip when it was time for him to leave.

"Hey son, you ready to catch this beat down?" Swerve kicked off his shoes and joined his son on the bed.

"You can't beat me," J.J. challenged.

"Aight, it's on then."

The two of them played the game until Yoshi called them for dinner. Being with his newfound family made Swerve anxious to put a baby in Rhapsodee. She wanted a family too, but she made it clear that she wasn't in a hurry. She let him know that she wanted to enjoy him before bringing any babies in the mix. Swerve washed his hands and then made his way to the dining room.

"Smells good babe," he took his seat.

Moments later, Yoshi sat a plate down in front of him and J.J. They said grace and devoured the shrimp and chicken alfredo, deep fried string beans, and garlic bread. Once they finished up eating, Swerve surprised himself by doing the dishes while Yoshi got J.J. ready for his bath. Once he was done, they all met in the living room and watched the Lion King. When it was over, it was almost ten and Swerve was ready to call it a night until Yoshi pulled him into the bedroom. He looked at her in the red negligee and his dick stood to attention right away. He was pretty sure if she wasn't already pregnant then she would have gotten pregnant within the past two weeks. Whoever said pregnant pussy was the best wasn't lying because Swerve was in love all over again.

"I'm horny daddy," Yoshi cooed.

Swerve didn't know his dick could get any harder, but after hearing those words, his shit really did. He stripped out of his clothes and gently pushed Yoshi back onto the bed. As much as he loved for his dick to be sucked, he didn't even have to have it at the moment. He was just ready to enter into her wetness. Apparently, Yoshi had other plans because she pushed him off of her and then released his dick from his Hanes boxers with the quickness. The way she wrapped her mouth around his whole dick had him ready to wife her.

"Yeah baby. Suck yo dick," Swerve gassed her up and the shit worked.

He felt himself getting ready to cum, so he pushed her up and then lifted her onto the bed. Even though he was ready to fuck, he decided to taste her a little bit to keep her satisfied. After she came in his mouth, Swerve raised up and entered into her wetness. The way she moaned and pulled him deeper, made him fuck the shit out of her. She tried to keep up with his pace, but it was no use. Swerve was fucking like he hadn't had sex in ages, and he had just made love to Rhap the night before. After Yoshi came again, Swerve released his seeds into her, falling down on the bed. He knew that he couldn't lay there long, but he did cuddle with Yoshi for a few minutes to satisfy her.

Since she was a light deep sleeper, Swerve laid there until she began snoring lightly and then made his exit. It was almost midnight when he got in the car. He prayed that Rhap decided to stay with Leah and the girls, but if not, he at least hoped to beat her home and take a shower. Traffic was light, so Swerve made it home in normal timing. He had been taking that route so much that his damn car should have been able to drive itself. Swerve's hopes dwindled when he pulled into the complex and saw Rhap's car. He parked and then his phone chimed with a text.

Yoshi: I thought you were staying. (mad face)

Swerve: I wish I could have, but now is not the right time babe.

Yoshi: I know I said I could handle this until the baby was born, but I'm not sure anymore.

Swerve: We gotta stick to the plan Yoshi, calm down and don't upset my baby.

Yoshi: Okay, but Swerve, don't play with me. I still think we gotta move the time frame up.

Swerve: We'll talk about it later.

Yoshi: I love you.

Swerve: Love you too.

Swerve knew that wasn't the end of the conversation, but he was happy that it was the end of it for the time being. After sitting there for a few more minutes, Swerve finally got out and headed inside. If luck was on his side, Rhapsodee would be asleep. That shit was short lived when he walked in and heard voices. Swerve stood there wondering why the hell she was back with company when she left to go and hang out with the girls.

"I appreciate you listening to me and not judging. I can't believe I got pregnant from a one-night stand. I feel so stupid," a woman sobbed.

"Shit happens girl. I'll be here for you and I'll even help you find the guy since you said it was a drunken night and you don't remember much."

Swerve walked in on their conversation and tried to walk straight through to get to the bedroom, but Rhap stopped him.

"Sorry babe. I planned on staying gone, but Sharon needed me. Remember I told you about her? I hate y'all are meeting under these circumstances, but Sharon, meet my husband Swerve, Swerve meet Sharon."

When Swerve locked eyes with Sharon, he dropped his keys. Even though he didn't sleep with her, he remembered her instantly because he woke up at her house the night that Rhap had caught him and Yoshi. He stood there trying to figure out when his wife had befriended the bartender.

"You okay babe?" Rhap broke him from his thoughts.

"Yeah, yeah, I'm good. Guess I had one too many drinks wit' Raymond."

"Nice to officially meet you Swerve. You seem like the type that can't hold your liquor," Sharon stood and shook his hand.

"Nice to meet you. Babe, I'ma let y'all finish up y'all girly shit. I'ma go and take a shower."

"Okay, hold on. Let me go to the bathroom real quick before you. Sharon, the other one is right down the hall," Rhap pointed and then went into the master bedroom.

"It's so good to finally meet my baby daddy," Sharon smirked.

"What the fuck are you talking 'bout?" Swerve hissed.

"Oh, you really don't remember what happened that night? Well, I have the video and I'll show you in due time, but just know that I don't plan on being a single mother," Sharon lied effortlessly.

"Bitch I don't know who you think I am, but you got me all the way fucked up. I'll…"

Before Swerve could finish his sentence, he heard Rhap coming back and was happy that she was singing some Keyshia Cole lyrics because that gave him a heads up.

"I'll be in touch," Sharon voiced and then sat down like nothing had happened.

Swerve headed to the bedroom, wondering what the fuck else could go wrong in his life.

Von Wiley Hall

Chapter Seventeen

Leah scrolled through Facebook and saw the different pictures from Myrtle Beach. She reminisced on the times that she was always there front and center, but her time had passed, and she laughed at the youngsters and their fun. Her phone vibrated and she clicked the text threads for the group chat with the girls. Leah doubled over in laughter at everyone, especially Twin as she talked about how she ended her sex drought for a nigga with a Vienna sausage. Another text came through and she hoped it was her new bae, but it was E-Love telling her to come by his place when she got off. It was a Friday evening, and she was surprised that he was at home. Leah couldn't lie, he had been extra attentive, but deep down she felt like she owed it to herself to explore things with Sebastian. She took her thoughts off, gathered her things, and then left the office for the day. She could have been gone, but she stayed there working ahead for some clients. E-Love's text was the motivation she needed to end the work week. She needed to talk to him anyway about ending their relationship.

Thirty minutes later, Leah pulled up at E-Love's place. It pained her to end things with him, but she had to do what she had to do since he wasn't ready for a committed relationship. Forcing some-one to be with her wasn't something that she had ever done, and she wasn't about to start that shit. Leah was a firm believer that a man knew exactly who and what he wanted. before she could knock on the door, it opened, and E-Love stood there in some black sweats and a wife beater and a white chef's hat. Her pussy had a mind of its own and started throbbing instantly when she looked down at his print. *Get it together girl. Stay strong. Don't be fooled by the dick,* she coached herself as she made her way inside.

Leah's mouth hit the floor when she walked in and saw rose petals on the floor and candles lit everywhere. She had never expe-rienced a romantic side from E-Love and silently wondered if he had a twin brother or some shit because the sight before her was totally out of character. If he would have been dressed in a suit or some shit, Leah would swear E-Love had been cloned.

"Ummm, who are you and what have you done with E-Love?" Leah cocked her head to the side.

"It's me baby. I just wanted some different shit, ya know," E-Love chuckled.

"I'm scared to ask any questions, so I'm just gon' go wit the flow," Leah marveled.

E-Love made his way towards the kitchen and Leah followed him. Once she saw the takeout bags from Perry's Seafood, she started laughing.

"See I was gon' cook, but I didn't have time so cut out all that laughing and shit. One day, I'ma cook for ya, for real, for real," E-Love told her.

"I'll believe it when I see it."

"Oh, you want me to throw this food away and cook?" he threatened.

"Hell naw, you know I love me some seafood. I hope you got extra crab legs and butter."

"That's what's in that bag by itself," he pointed.

"Ohhh let me find out you be paying attention to me and shit," Leah smirked.

"I pay attention to everything girl," E-Love walked up to her and pulled her close.

He lifted her chin and began kissing her passionately, and Leah welcomed his tongue. The butterflies that Leah hadn't felt in a few weeks for E-Love resurfaced like a wave pool. She had plans on ending whatever it was they had, but after seeing the other side to him, she had mixed feelings. E-Love picked her up and placed her on the counter, causing Leah to kick off her heels in the process. She felt E-Love unbuttoning her blouse and kissing on her chest.

"I wanna rip this shit off, but I'ma take my time," he said between kisses.

"You better not rip my shirt boy!"

"I got yo boy," he replied as she finished unbuttoning her shirt and then lifted her up again and removed her skirt.

"I thought w-we were bo-bout t-to eat?" Leah panted.

"We are, but I just wanna eat my meal first."

74

As soon as those words left his mouth, Leah felt E-Love's mouth on her clit. He inserted two fingers into her dripping wet pussy as his tongue massaged her clit. E-Love knew her body so well, and because of that, he made her cum almost instantly.

"Oh, my gawd," Leah screamed as her juices ran down her thighs.

E-Love continued feasting on her. He devoured her until she came again and before Leah could regain her composure, he entered his long, thick dick inside of her. She couldn't control the moans that escaped from her lips. Leah arched her back, triggering E-Love to go deeper. Leah threw it back at him as much as she could, but she knew that she was about to lose that battle. She was on her third orgasm and they were only ten minutes in. A few minutes later, E-Love went deeper than he ever been, and Leah knew that he was cumming by his grunts and the way his dick pulsated inside of her.

"What the hell was that? What's gotten into you? Now you got us both all sticky and shit," Leah faked an attitude, but in reality, she needed that shit and was happy as fuck.

"Shit, hell if I know, but I enjoyed every second of that shit. Let's go take a shower, then we can come back and eat," E-Love suggested.

Leah hopped down from the counter and almost fell, but E-Love caught her.

"Got my legs feeling like noodles and shit."

"That means I did my job," he boasted.

"Shut the hell up," Leah playfully punched him as they headed to take a shower together.

After sexing in the shower again, they finally got out and Leah put on one of E-Love's wife beaters and a pair of Polo boxers. He threw on a white tee and a pair of basketball shorts and they made their way back to the kitchen. After warming up the food and fixing their plates, Leah headed towards the living room where they always ate and watched TV, but E-Love stopped her and sat at the table.

"Ohhh, this is a date?" Leah purred.

"It is, now sit down and eat before I put some mo' act right up in ya!" he commanded.

"You lucky I'm ready to dive into this food," Leah rolled her eyes and sat down in the chair closest to E-Love.

They ate in silence for about five minutes. Leah could tell that E-Love wanted to say something, so she decided to help him out.

"What's on your mind, E-Love?"

"You," he simply replied.

"What about me?"

"You, me, us. I just been wondering what it would be like if I made shit official."

Leah was taken aback by his statement. That was absolutely the last thing that she thought he would say. E-Love had always been so adamant about not wanting to be in a relationship, and that was why Leah was willing to walk away. Leah knew what she wanted and that was someone of her own.

"It would be just like it is already, E-Love. I know how you feel, and that's why I've never tried to force you into shit, but you also know what I want. I'm too old to be playing games. Honestly, I was prepared to walk away from you today. I'm n..."

"For Mr. Irresistible huh?"

"Huh?" Leah coughed.

"Look Leah, I know I don't say it, but you should see it. I love yo ass," E-Love confessed.

Leah's ears had to be playing tricks on her, so she asked him to repeat himself.

"I said I love you. You know my life is complicated. That's why I never wanted to commit, but I'm willing to give it a try, if you are."

That was music to Leah's ears. She had been waiting to hear those words forever. She temporarily thought about Sebastian. Even though she was really feeling him, she knew that she was in love with E-Love.

"I love you too E-Love, and of course I'm willing to give it a try," she said as she fought back tears.

E-Love got up with Leah following suit. They shared a kiss, and the old flames were burning like never before.

BOOM!
BOOM!
BOOM!
BOOM!
BOOM!
BOOM!
"Open this muthafuckin' door, E-Love. Why doesn't my key work no more?" a female screamed from outside.

Leah glared up at E-Love and felt like everything that had just happened was a big ass mistake.

Von Wiley Hall

Chapter Eighteen

"Leah! Leah! Come on, bae. Leah, calm the fuck down and let me handle this shit," E-Love told her and headed towards the door.

"You gotta be fuckin' kidding me! Not even two seconds into this and we already got drama."

"Leah! I got this!" E-Love based as he stopped walking and told her before heading to the front door.

Before he could open the door, glass shattered, and Leah screamed. When he looked back at her, he noticed that a brick was beside her foot.

"Oh, whoever that bitch is, she just wrote a check her ass can't cash!" Leah rushed past him and he didn't even have time to grab her.

He ran out of the house behind her and saw her running down the driveway towards a car. Right before she could hop in the passenger's side, Leah grabbed the girl by the hair and slung her to the ground. While Leah beat the fuck out of her, E-Love made his way towards them, wondering how in the hell Simone even knew where he lived and why the fuck, she said anything about a key. He hadn't fucked with her since Leah beat her ass at Big Daddy's, so for her to pop up at his crib on some bullshit was beyond him. The girl who drove the car hopped out and acted like she was about to jump in the fight, but E-Love picked Leah up and dared the girls to jump stupid again.

"Put me the fuck down! I can't believe I sat there and fell for all that shit you was just talking," Leah kicked and screamed, but he didn't put her down.

It wasn't until she bit the shit out of him that he had no choice but to put her down because the shit hurt. She rushed into the house and he tried stopping her from grabbing her stuff, but it was no use. Leah wasn't hearing shit he had to say.

"Leah, I know how this shit looks, but I ain't never brought that bitch to my crib. You know I don't get down like that."

"E-Love, I really can't even be mad. I'm actually glad the shit happened now instead of later. We're done before we can even get started and I'm cool with that. You should be too. Just do what you been doing, and I'll finally start living my life. Deal?" Leah rolled her eyes and stepped around him after she put on a pair of his sweats that damn near swallowed her.

E-Love followed her outside and continued pleading with her, but they both stopped in their tracks when they noticed all of Leah's tires had been flattened. The situation just kept getting worse and the killer part was that he was really innocent and meant everything that he had said to Leah earlier.

"I'ma kill that bitch!" Leah spat.

"I'll make it right. I know you ain't tryna hear shit I got to say, but I'll take you home."

"Nah, I'm good. I'll Uber or see where my cousin at. You can go back in the house. Matter of fact go give yo girl a new key," she sarcastically instructed as she texted Rhap to come through and pick her up.

It was taking everything in E-Love to keep from saying fuck it. He was experiencing some feelings that he had never felt before, but he wasn't about to go out like no punk either. He pleaded with Leah until Rhap's car pulled up about ten minutes later. She ignored his ass and hopped in with the quickness. Rhapsodee must have been close by because there was no way in hell, she had made it from her place that quick. E-Love took his ass back in the house, feeling defeated as fuck. He had taken the night off just to chill with Leah and the shit turned out to be a disaster. E-Love went straight to his bar and grabbed the Cîroc. He removed the top and poured as much down his throat that he could hold at one time before swallowing it. His emotions started getting the best of him and he had a good mind to put Simone six feet under.

He shot Bobby B a text to see where he was because he needed his boy to talk to him off the ledge before he did something he might regret. While waiting on Bobby B to reply, his phone rang and he saw that it was his inspiration, his dad.

"What up, pops?" he answered and then poured some more Cîroc down his throat.

"What's going on son? Is everything straight in your area?'

"Business wise, it's all good."

"I sense a but. What's going on?"

"Man pops I think my ass done fell in love. Scratch that, I know I have," E-Love sighed.

"Wow, I must meet this young lady. You need to bring her to the cookout we're having next month," his dad advised.

Well, the thing is we just made out shit official tonight, but then some jump off popped up at my crib with some lies and everything went left not even five minutes later."

E-Love explained everything to his dad and his dad listened attentively. That was one of the things E-Love loved about his dad. He always listened and gave the best advice. E-Love didn't listen all of the time, but he knew his dad was a logical thinker and not a hot head, so he respected and valued his opinion whether he listened or not. After he finished explaining the situation, his dad simply said, "Find a way to get your girl, and if you love her like I believe you do, get rid of the jump-offs and make her your queen."

E-Love talked to his dad for a few more minutes and then laid back on the couch. The rest of the night consisted of him alone in his thoughts, thinking of a master plan.

Von Wiley Hall

Chapter Nineteen

"Are you gonna make a doctor's appointment anytime soon? If you're planning on keeping the baby, then it's best to go ahead and start your prenatal vitamins," Rhap said as her and Sharon were browsing through racks at Old Navy, looking at dresses.

"I'm still so torn. It's not that I'm against abortions, I really just don't know if I'll be able to live with myself for having one when I'm a grown ass woman and should have protected myself better," Sharon confessed.

"Shit happens, but I'll support whatever decision you make," Rhap replied.

She wanted to elaborate further but kept her thoughts to herself. She drifted back into deep thoughts about a decision she made years ago. Rhap still regretted lying on that table having an abortion, or it may have been the fact that Swerve found out that she regretted more. She wasn't really sure which one, but Rhap knew she didn't want kids at that moment because she was barely able to take care of herself. When Swerve forgave her for that, she vowed to give him a house full of babies once she was set in her career, and she felt like she owed it to him. That was one of the things that kept her holding on to her marriage.

"Rhapsodee, what's going on in your mind? You didn't hear a word I said," Sharon broke her from her reverie.

"Oh, my bad girl. What you say?"

"I was saying this color would look good on you."

"Oh, I actually ordered a dress in that color online last week. You buying that? I don't really see anything I want today," Rhap said.

"Hmmm, I was thinking about getting this, but it can wait. I need to get going, so I can get ready for work tonight. I missed last Friday, so tonight is a must," Sharon explained.

"Okay, I'll drop you back off at home and then I'm gonna go home and cook instead of eating out again."

They made their way out of the store and hopped into Rhap's car. As soon as Rhap turned into Sharon's complex, a text came through from Leah, asking Rhap to pick her up, and before she could reply, Leah had sent her location. Rhapsodee knew that it was E-Love's house when she saw the address because her cousin had shared her location before.

"I'll go with you to whatever appointment you make. Just let me know in advance," Rhap told Sharon and rubbed her hand before she got out.

Rhapsodee followed the directions to E-Love's house and pulled up ten minutes later. Leah was standing outside looking like she was ready to fight the world. She pretty much hopped in before Rhapsodee made a complete stop.

"Leah, what happened? I'm glad you called right after I dropped Sharon off because the last time y'all two were in the same room together, I don't even wanna relive it. But what happened though?" Rhap talked nonstop after Leah hopped in the passenger's seat with a scowl on her face.

"I really don't even wanna talk about it," Leah mumbled.

"Well, it's a good thing we ain't goin' off of your feelings because you 'bout to tell me why you so pissed off," Rhap retorted.

"Ugh!! Fuck that nigga!!" Leah let out a loud scream and then broke everything down to Rhap. Rhapsodee listened as her cousin gave her the rundown. She wanted to cut her off several times, but Rhap gave Leah the time she needed to vent. Once Leah was done, Rhap gathered her thoughts and then spoke.

"Have you lost your fucking mind, Leah? If you wouldn't have said anything about y'all having sex, I would think that you were on your period, but that's not the reason. So please tell me why you trippin' and letting a hoe like Simone ruin a relationship that you've been wanting for what seems like years!"

"Excuse me? You supposed to be on my side," Leah spat.

"I'm on the side of what's right and what's real, same way you get on me for Swerve's shit. I'm doing you the same way. Now me and you both know that E-Love might fuck around with these hoes, but to give a hoe like Simone a key ain't even his style. She probably been plotting and stalking. Didn't y'all get into a fight not long ago?"

"Yeah, but…"

"Ain't no buts Leah. You're overreacting and you not telling me the real deal." The car got silent before Rhap spoke again. "Oh, I get it. You really feeling this new man huh? He got you all sensitive and in your feelings? You don't even know him like you know E-Love, so please take that into consideration. He could be a woman-izer or…"

"He's nothing like that Rhap. He's mature and he knows what he wants. He knows I'm seeing someone and he even respects that. We are just getting to know each other while I figure out this thing with E-Love."

"You're defending him so yeah that's what this is all about. All I'm gonna say is just be careful. Everything that glitters ain't gold. I know I'm probably the last person that needs to be giving advice, but my cousin taught me to speak my mind, and I'm finally coming into myself," Rhap expressed.

Rhap continued driving while her cousin sat there in silence. There was more that Rhap wanted to say, but she decided to leave her in her own thoughts. That was what she needed at that moment, so Rhap obliged. She pulled up to their complex about thirty minutes later and parked.

"Thanks cousin. I'm about to go and take a nice hot bubble bath and get my shit together. I love you," Leah said and got out.

"I love you too cousin, and even though I got my own shit going on, you know I'm here for you."

Rhap sat in the car for a few minutes checking her email and pondering on her next assignment. She had been home a week or so before leaving. Rhapsodee learned money management skills at an early age in life because of how she struggled growing up. As a result, to that, she could go periods of time without working because of the money she made and still be okay. There were times when she was gone four to six weeks, so it was okay to be off a few weeks. She narrowed it down to three jobs and then made her way inside. Rhap went straight to the kitchen and poured herself a glass of wine so that she could relax and prepare for dinner. Swerve was at work, but he was scheduled to be off soon. There was a knock at the door and Rhap wondered who it could be. Figuring it must have been Leah, she opened the door without asking who it was and was faced by two cops.

"Rhapsodee St. John?" once cop questioned.

"Yes?"

"You're under arrest for the assault of Yoshi Brevardo. You have the right to remain silent. Anything you say can and will be used..."

Chapter Twenty

"Don't you think it's too early to buy baby stuff?" Swerve quizzed.

"Too early? You do realize I'm four months and we'll know what we're having at the next appointment right?" Yoshi shot back.

"I don't know anything about this kinda stuff," he admitted.

Swerve knew that he was wrong, but he was low-key excited about having a son and getting to be a part of the process of the new life he and Yoshi had created. He knew he had forgiven his wife for what she did, but it would be a lie if he said he didn't still think about it. Swerve knew that he couldn't continue living a double life, but he was damn sure going to try to get away with it for as long as he could. With Rhapsodee working away, it would be easier. The only way he was able to get away for the past week was because he had told her that he started a new job. He did get hired, but he wasn't scheduled to start until the next week.

"I understand. I'm sorry I didn't tell you about J.J. None of my family even knows who his dad is. Big Posse suspected it but I shut him down. We know that he gonna act a whole ass, but I'm happy that you're here now."

Instead of replying, Swerve continued looking at baby items while his mind wandered. Sharon popped into his mind and he had no idea what her angle was. He didn't remember sleeping with her at all, but she was adamant that they did. After he called her a bitch and liar the day after he saw her at his place, she sent a video of the two of them fucking on the couch. He looked out of it on the video, but she rode the hell out of his dick. Out of all the bullshit that he was caught up in, Swerve still wasn't willing to lose Rhapsodee. A bright idea popped into his head, and he hoped that he could pull it off.

Yoshi talked Swerve into getting some pampers, wipes, a bassinet, and a few more items. They left Wal-Mart and headed back to her house. It was almost time for J.J. to get out of school. Swerve planned on spending an hour or so with him before heading home. He knew that Rhapsodee was out with her fake ass friend. He hated it but felt like there wasn't shit he could do about it. After putting the bassinet together, Yoshi threw the pussy on him and they got cleaned up right before the bus dropped J.J. off. He told Swerve all about his day and the new friends that he had made as they played the game. Time flew by and before Swerve knew it, it was almost seven o'clock.

"I gotta get home. I'ma call you tomorrow," he told Yoshi as he grabbed his keys.

She started pouting, but Swerve couldn't fall for her tricks. He told Rhap that he had to work a little late, but he couldn't make it home too late and think everything would be okay.

"Can't you just…"

Swerve's phone rang while Yoshi was talking, and an unrecognized number popped up. Normally, he didn't answer numbers he didn't know, but since it was a local number, he went ahead and answered.

"You have a collect call from Rhapsodee. Do you accept the charges?" the automated recording stated.

"What the fuck? Yes, yes. I accept," he hurriedly agreed.

Swerve made his way out of Yoshi's apartment before the call connected. He heard her screaming, but he couldn't afford for Rhapsodee to hear her and was thankful that he already had his keys in his hands. He had no idea why Rhap would be calling from jail.

"You fuckin' cheated on me in our damn house and your bitch had the nerve to press charges on me?" Rhap spat once the call was connected.

"Wh-what? What you mean?" Swerve stuttered, not believing his ears.

He wanted to get out of his car and head back inside, but he needed to go and pick his wife up.

"You heard what I said. You better come and get me now. The only reason I'm calling you is because Leah didn't answer. Bail is $500!" Rhap hung up in his face.

Swerve made his way towards the bank so that he could get some money from the ATM because he only had about a hundred dollars in cash on him. After retrieving the money, he made his way to the jail, but he couldn't hold off on calling Yoshi any longer.

Hard and Ruthless

"Are you coming back babe?" she cooed.

"You had Rhap arrested?" he asked, already knowing the answer.

"Huh?"

"Bitch you heard wha..."

"Nigga if you ever call me a bitch again, I'll cut your fuckin' dick off. That was weeks ago. She beat my ass while I was pregnant, so you are damn right I pressed charges. It was before all this and I really thought the shit had been handled, but I don't regret the shit," Yoshi fumed.

"Yoshi, I'm sorry for calling you that. It'll never happen again, but you not helping our situation right now," Swerve pleaded in a much calmer voice.

She got quiet and he hoped that his words were registering.

"You gonna have to drop these charges if you want this transition to be smooth babe," Swerve sweet talked her.

"Okay," Yoshi sighed after a few moments of silence.

Swerve made it to the jail and parked, putting some change in the meter. He knew that Rhap was about to give him hell, so he braced himself for the madness and headed inside. It took three hours for them to process the paperwork for Rhapsodee to be released. Swerve was frustrated with the whole process, but his frustrations weren't a match for Rhap's anger. He would be dead if looks could kill by the death stare that she gave him after she rounded the corner. He had been trying to think of what he could say to her but kept drawing a blank mind. Rhap brushed past him and made her way outside and Swerve followed suit. He hit the locks on the car and Rhap got in before he made it to the car.

The ride home was silent and to Swerve, that was worse than arguing. He would have rather heard what she had to say so that he could deal with it, but her being silent meant that shit was about to get real. It hit him right then that he still had the memory loss card on his side, so he decided to give it a try.

"Babe, who had you arrested and why? I was tryna give you time to let me know something, but I'm confused as fuck," he finally broke the silence.

"Oh, let me guess. You still don't remember shit?" Rhap retorted.

"I swear I have no idea what's goin' on. Can you please fill me in?" Swerve pleaded.

"You know what? I don't even wanna talk about it. Just get me home and give me some time to think about what I need to do."

"What you mean? Do about what? If I did something, I'm truly sorry baby. I love you and I don't wanna lose you. If I can't remember something so bad, it must be a sign for us to move forward."

"When is your next appointment?" Rhap questioned.

"I'm not sure, why?"

"Don't worry 'bout it. I'll figure it out, but since you don't remember shit, just know that if I lose any potential jobs behind this bullshit, we're done!"

Swerve inwardly smiled because he already had that shit handled. He knew his time was running out with the memory shit, so he had to put his next plan into action.

Chapter Twenty-One

It had been a whole two weeks since the ordeal with E-Love and that bitch Simone, and Leah had managed to avoid E-Love at all costs. He had been persistent with his calls and texts, but Leah was thankful that he hadn't popped up. Deep down, she knew that it was only a matter of time before he did just that or said fuck it altogether. Leah was glad that her cousin was gone to work. Therefore, it was easy to keep from being face to face with her and hearing her mouth. Leah was sitting on the toilet staring at the fifth pregnancy test that she had taken in total disbelief. She grabbed her phone and pulled up the iPeriod app for the hundredth time, and once again, it said that her cycle was twenty-three days late.

"These shits gotta be wrong. I gotta go buy some more," she mumbled to herself.

Leah had ignored the symptoms, chucking them up to things that she had been eating. As she sat there, she was still in denial. She finally got up, hopped in the shower with a mind to go to Wal-Mart to grab some more pregnancy tests. She had the EPT brand, but there had to be something more expensive with better results. Thoughts of Sebastian filled Leah's mind and she knew that if she was indeed pregnant, that relationship would also be over before it got started. After washing and rinsing off a few times with her exfoliating Dove body wash, Leah got out and dried off. She got dressed in a pair of Nike tights and pink Nike tee that matched her light cream rose Air Max 97's. She released the rubber band from her braids and let them hang down her back, grabbed her phone and purse, and headed for the door. As soon as she twisted the knob and prepared to exit, her breath was caught in her throat at the sight of E-Love.

"What are you doin' here? What you want Eric?" Leah asked, calling him by his government name and trying to fight through her emotions.

"Step to the side, Leah," he matched her tone and walked in with a dozen yellow roses, balloons, and candy.

Leah had no choice but to step to the side or he would have knocked her ass over. He went and placed the items he had on her mirror table that was in the middle of the living room and then took a seat on the couch like he owned the place.

"We're doing pop ups now?" Leah inquired after she closed the door.

"I gave you enough time to be all mad and shit, for no fuckin' reason might I add/ Now it's time to talk like adults," E-Love entreated.

Leah thought about the pregnancy tests that she had left lying all over the bathroom floor. E-Love wasn't the snooping type, but she had left the shit everywhere. She ran to the bathroom and threw everything under the counter. To keep from having to give an explanation for that, she decided to give E-Love what he wanted, a conversation.

"Okay E-Love, what is it that you have to say?" she expressed nonchalantly as she stood near the love seat that was adjacent to the couch.

"You wanna go get something to eat?"

"No."

"Damn. Well listen. I got down to the bottom of that shit. That crazy bitch was on some stalker type shit. I ain't fucked around with her since before that time you beat her ass. I guess she was in her feelings and was on some get back type shit. I meant everything I said to you. I love you, but I ain't no beggin' ass nigga. I feel like I done gave you enough time to get over this bullshit, but if you need one more week, I'll allow it. To show you how serious I am, I wanna take you to meet my family next weekend. Be sure you open that box before you leave," E-Love said his peace, got up, kissed Leah on the forehead, and then left out just as quickly as he came.

Leah stood there speechless. E-Love was saying all of the right things. It was everything that she had been dying to hear, but she was scared as hell. When she walked towards the table, her phone rang, and she knew that it was her mom by the ringtone. She had been avoiding her mom's calls because her mom could always tell when something was going on, and Leah really didn't want to reveal anything at that moment. Since she had missed so many calls, she had to answer so that her parents wouldn't be worried.

"Hi mom, don't fuss. Work has been really busy these past couple of weeks," Leah tried to smooth things over as soon as she answered.

"Leah, the only time you avoid my calls is when something is wrong, so spill it."

"I'm fine mom. Really, I am," Leah tried convincing herself more than her mom.

There was a long moment of silence. Leah knew all too well that her mom was waiting on her to open up.

"Okay, there's this one thing that I had going on, but I finally got it figured out, so I really don't even have to relive it," Leah explained.

"Well good, so when are you coming to visit? And are you gonna give us some grandbabies before we die?" her mom bluntly asked, and Leah went into a coughing fit.

"Mooommm, don't talk like that. Y'all not about to die no time soon."

"We can't live forever, and...never mind. When are you visiting? You didn't answer that question and be sure to bring your man with you."

"What were you about to say mom? I'm planning on coming there very soon. Is everything alright?" Leah became concerned.

She heard her mom talking to someone, but it was muffled because her hand was over the phone.

"Baby let me call you back okay. I love you and we want to see you soon. Christmas was three months ago."

"I love y'all too mom and I'll get there for Memorial Day."

Her mom told her okay, but Leah heard the sigh. As soon as she hung up, she pulled up the Travelocity app and booked a flight for a week during Memorial Day. Leah always flew down to Florida for the main holidays and she hadn't missed one, so she didn't know why her mom was acting like she had. Her parents were old though, and she knew that she needed to get down there more often. Since Memorial Day was at the end of the next month, she figured all would be fine and then proceeded to pick up the box that E-Love mentioned. It was in the middle of the arrangement. She opened the box and saw a car key. Leah couldn't stop the smile that formed on her lips as she made her way to the window and looked out. A red bow was on a black 700 series BMW. A single tear slid down her face because she mentioned how that was going to be her next car to Rhapsodee and E-Love bought it. She put her pride to the side and dialed his number.

Chapter Twenty-Two

A few minutes after E-Love left Leah's, D'Lamar hit his line with some shit he didn't want to hear. He made his way towards the warehouse with his mind in a million places. In the game, niggas could switch up at any given time, but when it was done by someone that had been loyal from day one, the shit cut deep. E-Love knew that if D'Lamar said it, then it was true, but deep down, he still hoped that it was some kinda mistake. It took no time at all for E-Love to make it to his destination since he was already headed to that spot when D'Lamar called. The shit wasn't a coincidence either. He pulled up to the spot, checked his surroundings out of habit, and then went inside.

When E-Love walked in, he saw Moon strapped to a chair in the middle of the floor. Moon had been with the crew from the very beginning. E-Love never wanted to know the reasons why a nigga crossed him, but he felt like he needed to know. Before any words were spoken, D'Lamar walked up to him and handed him his phone. E-Love hit play on the video and watched the entire five minutes in disbelief. Once it was over, he stood there and thought back over the years on how he always looked out for Moon and how he thought the shit had been reciprocated, but evidently, he had missed some shit along the way.

E-Love walked up to pull the tape from his mouth. He tried to think of exactly what he wanted to say. He knew what to say but couldn't figure out how to say it.

"I'm sorry man," Moon mumbled.

"Sorry ain't enough, my nigga. You went against the grain. You had the balls to follow me and Bobby B to Birmingham, and then you were in car with them niggas that shot at us?" E-Love shook his head in disgust.

A single tear slid from E-Love's right eye, but he had no choice but to pull his gun, sending a single dome shot to one of his best friends. He walked off and gave D'Lamar the signal, knowing his other boy knew exactly what to do. E-Love left and got back in his car. He reached under the seat and grabbed the bottle of Vodka that he had bought the day before. Just when he was about to open it, he stopped. Even though he wanted to down half the bottle, he knew the chances of getting stopped by the police was already great and he didn't need those type of problems. Instead, he put the bottle back and decided to just head to the gun range. He needed a stress reliever. In the past, he would call Leah and be okay. E-Love never admitted the shit to her, but he would always call when he was dealing with some shit, and Leah made it better just because of who she was. E-Love started his vehicle, shifted into gear, and pulled away. Not even thirty seconds into his drive, his phone rang, and he was surprised as hell to see that it was Leah calling. Her ass was stubborn, and he didn't expect her to even consider calling for a few more days.

"Hello," he answered.

"I'm sorry I overreacted and you're right. I do wanna meet your family and see where this relationship can go. I love you E-Love."

E-Love released a breath that he didn't even know that he was holding until after she had finished talking. Leah had him feeling shit that he had never felt before, and E-Love didn't know if that was good or bad.

"Mind if I come back over?" he asked.

"I don't mind," Leah replied.

With that being said, E-Love headed back to Leah's condo in hopes that he could relieve his stress in another way.

Chapter Twenty-Three

Right before Rhap left for her last work assignment, she confronted Swerve about his memory loss shit because the doctor made it clear that he should have been fine or they would have to give him a different medication to reverse it. He had no choice but to come clean because of the side effects that were mentioned. All of that was a result to Rhapsodee confiding in the doctor about her suspicions because she had grown sick of the bullshit. Being arrested by his side chick had already pissed her off, and Rhap told Swerve that he better do whatever the fuck he needed to do to fix the situation. It infuriated Rhap so bad, that she left the next day, putting his number on block for the whole two weeks that she was gone. It was the Thursday before Easter and Rhap would have worked longer if she would have known that Leah was going to be out of town. She also knew that her mom was expecting her to drive to her house for dinner, and Rhap was excited about that, except for the fact that Swerve may want to go.

Rhapsodee made a couple of stops and then headed home. Normally, she would get groceries, but she told herself that Swerve could fend for his damn self. It was about four o'clock when Rhap made it home, and she hoped that she would have a couple of hours by herself. Her cramps were getting the best of her, and she wasn't in the mood for any bullshit, so prayerfully, Swerve was still at work. She thanked God when she didn't see his car in its normal space. She circled around and parked in the back where she knew some vacant spaces were because they were actually closer to the door. After grabbing her things, Rhap made her way inside and began her unpacking. She saw the kitchen was spotless and that shocked the shit out of her because Swerve normally kept a mess. Even though that was out of the norm, she was happy that she didn't have to add that to her list.

An hour later, Rhap was out of the shower and putting on a pair of her favorite pajamas. She grabbed her takeout bag from Ralph and Kacoos, hopped in the bed, and started where she left off on binge watching Empire. Rhap wasn't a regular TV watcher, but her coworkers always talked about certain shows, and she took their recommendations and had been a binge watcher of different shows for the past few months. Two episodes in, Rhap heard Swerve's voice and rolled her eyes.

"It was a rough day and I'm tired so nah I can't make it. Look, I'm tired as fuck and…"

Swerve walked in and hung up the phone mid-sentence when he saw Rhap.

"Baby I-I'm glad you're home. I can send this text and set this appointment for tomorrow," Swerve said and came towards the bed.

"Who were you talking to? You know what, never mind. I don't even wanna know," Rhap held up her hand and pushed him back once he got close.

"It was Big Posse wanting me to come to the bar. I had…"

"So, you just hung up on Big Posse like you can't talk to him in front of me?" Rhap rolled her eyes.

"I can call him right back if you want."

"I really don't give a fuck Swerve," Rhap hissed because just the sight of him had put her on ten.

"I'm sorry baby. Please let's go to this counseling session tomorrow, so I can get my true feelings out there. I only lied because I didn't wanna lose you and I still don't want to," Swerve confessed. "We took vows and we said for better or worse," he continued when she didn't respond.

"Oh, so now you wanna throw the vows in there?"

"I fucked up and I just wanna make it right. That's all I'm saying babe. Please, let's go to counseling tomorrow so we can get back on the right track," Swerve pleaded.

"Go sleep in the other room, Swerve. I don't wanna be next to you. Actually, it'll be better for you than it will for me. Get everything you need," she stated and then turned back into her show.

She was still confused as fuck about everything. Rhap couldn't lie and act like she didn't love her husband because she did. However, she was tired of being the one to look over everything to find the good in every situation. She got up and locked the bedroom door after Swerve left and turned the TV off. Rhap said a long prayer, tossing and turning for about an hour before she drifted off to sleep.

The next morning, there was a light tap at the bedroom door. Rhap grabbed her phone off of the nightstand and saw that it was a quarter to nine. Swerve should have been gone to work, but there he was. She hesitantly got up and unlocked the door and then made her way to the bathroom so that she could handle her hygiene.

"The counseling session is set up for ten thirty babe. I'll be ready and waiting," Swerve cajoled from the other side of the door. She expected him to come in the room but was elated that he didn't.

Forty-five minutes later, Rhap was dressed in a pair of blue jeans she bought from Gap and a pink V-neck tee shirt. Her hair was in a high, sloppy bun and after she put on some lip gloss, she was ready to go. After thinking long and hard, Rhap made the decision to do all that she could do to make her marriage work. If the shit didn't work, she knew that she was going to be done with love, but deep down, she wasn't ready for that. When Rhap walked into the living room, Swerve was sitting on the couch with his eyes closed and his hands in the praying position. Had it been any other day, the gesture would have melted Rhap's heart. He must have felt her presence after a few seconds because he stood up and Rhap noticed that he was dressed in a suit.

"We gotta wear Sunday's best for counseling?" she quizzed.

"I just want to show you how serious I am."

Rhap thought about changing, but she was dressed for her mood and that was that. They made their way out of the door and Rhap followed Swerve to his car. She thought about driving and trailing him, but figured if she was going to make an honest try, then she had to be all in. Swerve tried making small talk, but he finally stopped after she continued giving him one-word answers. Rhap wanted to ask where they were attending counseling, but since she had been so short with Swerve, she decided to just wait it out. They arrived at their destination about twenty minutes later, and Rhap sighed and said a silent prayer that everything would go well.

It wasn't even fifteen minutes into the session and the words that Swerve spoke had Rhap feeling like shit. She never knew that her being gone made her husband feel neglected. He wasn't speaking in a way that made her feel bad and that was the killing part. Swerve owned up to his shit and seemed to be sincerely pouring his heart out. The part that stung the worst was when he talked about the abortion she had and how he felt like he lost a piece of himself.

"What are you feeling right now?" Dr. May asked Rhapsodee.

"I honestly feel like shit. Although I still hate the fact that he cheated. I know that I have to take some responsibility for it," Rhap confessed.

"Do you both want your marriage to work?"

"I do. I love my wife so much. I know I have to work a thousand times harder to gain her trust back, and I'll do just that. I don't want her to feel bad about her job anymore. I just have to make an effort to meet her halfway. I've made so many mistakes, but I'll do everything I can to make it up to her for the rest of my life."

"And what about you Rhapsodee?"

"I do. I'm gonna do everything I can to make my marriage work. Someone reminded me that it's for better or worse. Our good days have outweighed the bad, so I owe it to Swerve to give it my all. If that means getting a job at home, then I'll do that."

"I know you love traveling, baby. I fucked up, but I don't want you unhappy. I can start visiting you wherever you're at. You don't have to work here. I don't want you to resent me for it."

"We can talk about it," Rhap replied.

The therapist asked them a few more questions and then had them do some more exercises with each other and surprisingly, they did all of them well.

"You two are going to be just fine. You've made more progress in one session than a lot of my clients have made in months. I'd like to see you all back in two weeks together if your schedule allows it," Dr. May stated.

Rhapsodee and Swerve walked out of the office hand in hand, feeling refreshed. Rhap still had a small feeling of doubt in the back of her mind like something was wrong, but she decided to let it go for the moment, telling herself that whatever was meant to be would be.

Chapter Twenty-Four

Swerve was happy as fuck. He really did mean what he said, but he was more excited that his home girl was able to play the therapist role so well. She had to have been a Googling ass to know what type of marriage questions to ask. The role reversal game even turned out to be good because of the questions that were asked afterwards. Swerve opened Rhap's car door for her and then went around and hopped in the driver's seat after she was inside.

"What you got a taste for?" he asked as he started the car.

"Hmm, it doesn't matter. What you want?"

"You," he smirked.

"Wellll, that won't be happening for a few more days, so pick something wise," Rhap replied.

At first, Swerve thought that she was just turning him down until she said a few days. Yoshi had been sexing him like crazy, so waiting a few days wasn't going to hurt anything. The thought of Rhap finding out about Yoshi was painful. That's why he was going to do everything that he could to make sure that both women were happy for as long as he possibly could.

"I'll make up for lost time in a few days. Let's go to Morrison's since it's nearby," Swerve suggested.

Three hours later, Rhap was lying down for a nap and Swerve told her that he had to go and run a few errands. The only thing she wanted back was some strawberry ice cream and he assured her that he would get them on his way back in. Everything felt like old times to Swerve, and he hoped that Rhap was feeling the same way. As soon as Rhap had been asleep for a few minutes, Swerve dipped out and headed to the bank. One thing that he was happy about, him and Rhap had a joint account as well as separate accounts. He was surprised that she hadn't ever said anything about putting all of their money together, but he was happy. Swerve withdrew enough money to cover Yoshi's rent and then went by Burger King, grabbing both her and J.J. something to eat and then made his way to Lithonia. Yoshi had been blowing him up since he dipped out on her the night before. Swerve was glad that he followed his first mind and went home. Rhap hadn't been telling him when she would be coming and going, which was understandable, and him going home had worked out in his favor.

Swerve's phone rang and he looked at it and noticed that it was Sharon. He still didn't remember fucking her, but she was adamant about carrying his child.

"What up?" he answered.

"You gon' stop playing me to the left before I tell your little wife what's going on," Sharon spat.

"You know what, I'm not 'bout to be playing these games with yo ass. I'm scheduling you an appointment for Monday, so we can confirm this shit and then we gon' get a DNA test while you are pregnant. Yo trick ass befriended my wife and now you want a baby by me? What kinda sick shit is that?" Swerve fumed.

"You ain't gon' talk to me any kinda..."

"I'll text you the details," Swerve said and hung up as he pulled up to Yoshi's place.

He used his key and let himself inside once he arrived. Yoshi was sitting at the kitchen table reading over something.

"Hey babe," he tried smoothing things over ahead of time.

"Don't hey babe me. Yo brought me a Whopper, but where my fries at?" Yoshi rolled her eyes.

"The fries. Shit, I forgot them," he shrugged.

Swerve sat the money on the table and Yoshi snatched it up real quick.

"What about the money for me dropping the charges? You offered," she reminded him with a mouth full of fries.

"That's all I can spare this week. If we gon' be together, we gotta move different, Yoshi. I know I offered the money, but with me being your man and all, you shoulda never agreed to accept it. You can't do shit to stress me and push me away ma. Come on now. We gon' make this shit work, but I can't take the nagging."

"Okay baby. I'll try to do better. You know I'm all emotional and shit, but I'll make an effort. You got some shit you gotta work on too," Yoshi expressed.

"Well we'll talk about all that later. I don't have much time so how 'bout you come work some magic with them lips before J.J. gets here," Swerved beseeched.

Before they could make it to the room, there was a knock at the door and Yoshi started walking towards it.

"Wait, who is that?" Swerve quizzed.

"It's probably my brother. He supposed to be dropping a game off for J.J."

"Damn Yoshi, he probably saw my car," Swerve became worried.

"Well you didn't call before you came and he gotta find out sooner or later anyway," Yoshi shrugged before she went and opened the door.

Swerve didn't understand why Yoshi was so calm. She knew how shit fell apart years ago. Before he could take another step, Big Posse was inside and the look that he gave Swerve was a death stare.

"We might as well get this shit over with. Big Posse, I been lying to you. Swerve is J.J.'s dad and he's also the father of the other child I'm carrying. We're gonna be a family, and I hope you're okay with it," Yoshi put it all out there.

Big Posse ran up on Swerve and hit him with a right hook before he could do anything.

"You a dirty motherfucker man!" Big Posse spat and left just as fast as he came.

Swerve felt like his jaw was broken, and that was why he couldn't react. Yoshi made him an ice pack and sucked his dick while apologizing over and over and over. Swerve was pissed but a little relieved because at least that was one less person that he had to lie to.

Von Wiley Hall

Chapter Twenty-Five

Leah was nervous, excited, scared, and probably every emotion that you could think of. The past week between her and E-Love had been absolutely amazing. She still hadn't told him that she was pregnant because deep down, she still didn't believe it herself. In fact, she hadn't told anyone, not even Rhap or Twin. While sitting at the office, Leah decided to hit up the group chat and possibly break the news to her girls.

Leah: What y'all doing?

Twin: Hey trick, nothing much right now.

Princess: Cleaning up.

Rhap: I'm headed to eat with Swerve. I'll catch up on these texts later because we're pulling up at the spot now.

Leah: (eye rolling emoji)

Twin: Be nice trick. What you doing?

Leah: I gotta tell y'all something.

Leah: And y'all better keep it in this chat!!!

Twin: Oh shit, what you do now? I thought you and E-Love was good.

Princess: Did you beat that girl up again Leah?

Leah: We are GREAT Twin, I'm meeting the family tomorrow and NO Princess LOL!

Leah: But listen, I think I'm pregnant. Well I don't think it, but all of the test I took think I am.

Twin: Whatttt? E-Love tapped that ass real good, I betcha he went down and got him a girl too. Congrats! I'm about to be an auntie.

Princess: Pregnant? Girl hush ya mouf! Better you than me cousin, congrats. But I see you in denial.

Leah: Don't be saying no damn congrats. I don't need to be pregnant right now.

Twin: It is what it is, I'm happy for you and you know I'm gonna love being an aunt. Girl, you know your ass ain't fixin' to go through this alone.

Princess: You made a doctor's appointment?

Leah: *No, but I will soon. My client is here y'all. I'll get back with y'all later.*
Twin: *Bet.*
Princess: *Okay.*

Two hours later, Leah had everything organized for her clients and they walked out of her office together. Leah headed towards StoneCrest Mall so that she could pick up a few items she saw online the night before. She wanted to make a good impression on E-Love's family and found the perfect outfit and purse while surfing the internet. I-20 was packed as usual, but Leah was glad that she was beating the five o'clock traffic. The hot light was on at Krispy Kreme and it took everything in her not to bust that U-turn. She made it to the mall and parked by the Macy's entrance and was in and out in twenty minutes.

Even though the line was long as hell at Krispy Kreme, Leah had to stop. Those donuts melted in your mouth when you caught the hot light on. The line moved pretty fast and she had her donuts and was headed home within ten minutes. Her and E-Love were leaving the next morning at about nine thirty. He assured her that even though they were black, his family didn't operate on CP time because they liked to have fun twenty-four seven. They were scheduled to start at noon, so they would get there pretty much on time.

During the drive home, Leah called her mom and caught up with her. She really couldn't wait until the next month so that she could go and see them. Leah had been contemplating flying down before that for a couple of days and then going back for a whole week like she planned. Her dad had been sleeping the last few times she talked to her mom, so before she hung up, Leah made her mom promise to have him call. Leah pulled up at her complex and saw Swerve leaving. She wanted to flip his ass off, but instead, she ignored him and went on about her way. He probably didn't know it was her because she was in her new car. E-Love had gone above and beyond for her. He even had her name engraved in the steering wheel. Everything was just perfect, and she couldn't wait to make more memories with her man. She headed home for a night of self-pampering since E-Love had already told her that he would be busy after the funeral and repast of a close friend.

The next morning, Leah rolled over and E-Love pulled her back. He had come over to her place after all, and of course their phenomenal lovemaking sessions continued. It was like E-Love couldn't get enough of her and the feeling was mutual.

"Come on and let me get some of that good good before we get dressed," E-Love began kissing her neck.

"Oh, so you just can't get enough huh?" Leah smiled.

"Hell naw, now come climb on top," he pulled her up.

Leah didn't waste any time doing just what E-Love said. He raised up and kissed her nipples one at a time and her juices started flowing instantly. Since they both slept in their birthday suits, Leah felt E-Love's dick as it grew longer and harder. She raised up and slid down slowly on his pole.

"Ahh," she moaned as he stretched her.

Leah glided up and down slowly, savoring each moment. Her eyes rolled to the back of her head each time E-Love lifted up and hit her spot. She squeezed her pelvic muscles tight and E-Love gripped her ass and then flipped her over, gaining control.

"I'm winning today," he said as he lifted both of her legs over his shoulder and went as deep as he could. Leah started squirting and she knew that shit turned him on even more. She tried to match his pace, but it was no use. He was about to win that round and Leah didn't even care. After E-Love made her cum again, she felt his dick pulsating and he barely pulled out before his come spilled out on her stomach.

Too late for that shit, Leah thought to herself.

An hour later, they were both dressed and ready to hit the road right on schedule. Leah pulled E-Love back in front of her floor length mirror and snapped a few pictures and then a couple of selfies. He had never been the picture taking type, but he didn't complain, and that simple gesture made her love him even more. They made their way outside and E-Love headed to Leah's car.

"I didn't get to test drive this baby like I wanted to, so I'll do that today," he said, opening the driver's door after she hit the unlock button.

"Fine with me." She got comfortable in the passenger's seat and started posting some of the pictures that she had just snapped.

A text came through a few minutes after Leah put her phone down, and she fought to keep a calm demeanor on the outside. Her insides were tingling.

Mr. Irresistible: I know you said this isn't what you want, but I really did enjoy the time we spent together. Let me have you for one more weekend, and if you still want to call it quits, I'll take my losses and walk away.

Leah had broken things off with Sebastian. It was the first time that he had reached out to her since she ended their little thing. Leah was tempted to text back, but she didn't. Her being pregnant was probably the only reason that she didn't.

"Sooo who's the last person you took to meet you mom?" Leah quizzed after sitting her phone back down.

"Nobody has ever met my mom in my adult life. That prom shit back in high school don't count, do it?" he replied.

"Hmmm, nah I suppose that don't count. You think she gon' like me?

"Time will tell," he laughed, and Leah reached over and hit his shoulder. "Nah but for real, she will. You're real and my OG can tell the real from the fake right away. You stuck with me now girl. Got me doing shit I ain't never did."

"Ain't nothing wrong with change," she giggled.

E-Love stopped for gas and bought Leah a few snacks to hold her over. They talked a little and listened to music and in no time, E-Love was pulling up to their destination. Leah began to get nervous and she really wasn't the type to let other people's opinions get to her, but that time, it was different. E-Love must have noticed the change because he reached over and grabbed her hand.

"I know damn well Miss Leah ain't letting nobody make her sweat. Calm down girl and come on."

Leah laughed and hit him again. She didn't know why she expected some sentimental shit from him. He was being nice, but he was still himself. There were cars everywhere and Leah could tell right away that E-Love's house had to be the go-to house. They got out and made their way to the back yard. E-Love introduced her to a few of his cousins first and this his sister. Surprisingly, her and Leah hit it off right away and Meek took over E-Love's job and started introducing her to everyone.

Leah and Meek partnered up and started playing spades. They were on their third hand when E-Love came and grabbed her.

"E-Love what you doing? We 'bout to run a wheel on these clowns!" Meek fussed.

"Just pause that shit. She'll be right back."

They made it to the kitchen and Leah finally met the lady who had given E-Love life. She was so beautiful that Leah was speechless. She didn't know what she expected, but E-Love's mom was the same complexion as her and her hair was down her back.

"So I finally get to meet the beautiful lady that keeps my son from coming home every weekend now," Marian pulled her in for a hug.

"It's nice to meet you, but I can't take all the credit for him not coming home. He does his own thang," Leah replied, sharing a laugh with his mom.

They talked like they had known each other forever and Leah was finally fully relaxed. Meek busted in the door and fussed at Leah for ditching her, so Leah excused herself to go back outside. E-Love followed behind with a Bud Light in his hand.

"You want a drink?" he asked her.

"Nah, I'm good babe."

Her and Meek resumed their game, winning the hand. E-Love grabbed up one of his cousins and they started a new game against them.

"Damn, I left my phone in the house. Let me use your phone to see where my dad is?" E-Love asked Leah.

"Your dad coming? I thought him, and your mom wasn't together anymore," Leah said as she handed him the phone.

"They not, but they still get along and shit and he always come to family functions," E-Love shrugged.

It wasn't Leah's business, so she didn't say shit else. She began setting her hand, but the words that left E-Love's mouth caused her to drop all of her cards.

Chapter Twenty-Six

"Mr. Irresistible? So, you mean to tell me my fuckin' father is Mr. Irresistible?" E-Love fumed after he noticed what name was saved for the number he dialed.

He stared at the phone again and saw that it had connected, putting it on the speaker.

"You changed your mind, darling?" his dad asked.

E-Love ended the call and saw Leah visibly shaking. Out of the corner of his eye, he saw his dad standing near the entrance to the backyard. Before he could stop himself, E-Love was halfway to his dad and had no idea that the entire backyard was following him.

"E-Love, E-Love, wait a minute! I didn't know!" Leah screamed in the background, but he ignored her for the moment.

"Hi son," his dad greeted, unaware of the situation that was unfolding.

"You fuckin' my girl?" E-Love based.

"Boy you better watch how the fuck you talk to me and what the hell are you talking about?" his dad's voice matched his.

At that moment, Leah stood beside E-Love and the facial expression that took over his dad's face told him everything that he needed to know.

"E-Love, I didn't know Sebastian was your dad, baby. Oh my God! I really had no idea," Leah pleaded.

"Son, I really had no idea!"

"Y'all expect me to believe this bullshit?" E-Love spat.

"Didn't I just tell you to watch how you talk to me?" Sebastian stepped to him and grabbed him by the shirt.

"Because you my Pops, I'ma let you live, but fuck both of y'all! I'm out!" E-Love exploded and walked away.

"Son. come back here!" his dad shouted after him.

"What's going on out here?" Marian called out.

E-Love made it to the front and that was when he realized that he drove Leah's car and had given her the keys to put in her purse. If he would've had them in his pocket, he probably would have left and not thought shit about it. E-Love went in the front door and grabbed his mother's keys right off the table and left back out. He didn't know where he was going, but he knew that he had to get the fuck away from there.

"E-Love, wait. Please listen to me," Leah caught up with him before he got in the car.

"I don't have a muthafuckin' thang to say to you. Go back there and talk to Mr. Irresistible. Can't believe I was really 'bout to wife up a…"

"Call me a hoe and I'ma fight you like a nigga out here in these streets!" Leah interrupted him, stepping closer.

"Look, it's best for me to just leave, and I advise you to be gone before I get back," E-Love hopped in the car and cranked up. He drove away with Leah still standing there.

Since there was a liquor store on pretty much every corner, it didn't take E-Love long to pull up at one. He went and grabbed some Grand Marnier and a Coke. On the way out, he bumped into Maya, the one girl that had met his mom on his senior prom night.

"Well, well, well, if it isn't the infamous Eric. Oh wait, you only go by E-Love now, right?" she smiled.

"What's up Maya?'

"You," she simply replied.

"Gone girl," E-Love chuckled and tried to walk around her, but she blocked his path.

"Come on E-Love. That was years ago. Give me a chance to make it up to you," Maya grabbed his dick.

The thought of the head that she used to give made his penis grow hard.

"See, he misses me," she smirked.

With everything that had just happened, some pussy would help for the moment. E-Love couldn't even describe his feelings, but he knew that he didn't like the shit.

"Meet me at the Marriott in thirty. I'll leave the room number at the front desk," E-Love told her and walked away.

Almost a whole bottle and an hour later, E-Love's dick was deep down Maya's throat. He didn't know why he didn't turn his phone completely off because the constant vibration of it was killing the fucking vibe.

"Ummm, do you need to get that?" Maya asked.

"Nah girl, why you stop and ask that?"

"Because clearly something is wrong. Yo dick ain't even hard no more."

"Fuck," E-Love mumbled.

"Thought I was finna get some dick," Maya grumbled.

She started gathering her shit and left before E-Love could say anything. He fell back onto the bed, closed his eyes, and rubbed his temples. He had no idea how shit could be so kosher one minute and then fucked up beyond repair the next. E-Love got up and downed the rest of the liquor and then passed out on the bed.

Von Wiley Hall

Chapter Twenty-Seven

Things for Rhap and Swerve had been feeling like the good ol' days. She was finally letting her guards down just a little. She wasn't going to be stupid or anything, but if she wanted her marriage to work, Rhap knew that she had to truly forgive and move forward. Rhap was on her laptop searching for jobs close to home. Even though Swerve told her that he understood her working away, she still decided to make an honest effort to see what was worth applying for close by. Rhap decided to take a break from job searching because nothing seemed too appealing to her. A Gerber commercial came on and it made Rhap think of Leah and Sharon. It made her think briefly about having kids. It was weird to her that Swerve hadn't brought up the subject in a while, but she was relieved because she still wasn't sure that they were ready. The shit that they had been going through really confirmed to her that shit wasn't solid, and Rhap was thankful there weren't any kids involved.

Swerve was in the kitchen cooking dinner, which surprised Rhap, but she wasn't complaining. Normally, he would be hanging out with Big Posse on a Saturday evening, but he was at home and appeared to be happy. Rhap figured he must have still been feeling a little pain from the punch he took after breaking up a fight at the store. She tried to get him to go to the emergency room because he had been complaining about a headache for days, but he was adamant that the Tylenol extra strengths he was taking would do. Rhap made her way to the kitchen and Swerve stood at the stove with his back turned.

"Smells good in here," she said, startling Swerve.

"Damn you scared me girl," he nervously stated.

"You've been extra jumpy. Are you sure you're okay?" Rhap queried.

"Yeah babe. I'm good. You hungry? I'm almost done."

"Yess, I can't wait to dive in."

Rhap's phone rang and she was surprised to see that it was Leah calling since she was away meeting E-Love's family.

"Hey cousin! You need me to come and whoop somebody ass?" Rhap joked.

Rhap heard some sniffles and knew that Leah was crying. That instantly made her cut her joking out because Leah wasn't the crying type.

"Leah, what's wrong? Where are you?"

"I'm almost at home. Can you come over when you get time?" Leah said barely above a whisper.

"Of course, I'll use my key and head over now, so I can be there when you make it," Rhap told her and hung up.

She went and slipped into her slides since they were right beside the bed and prepared to head out.

"Sorry babe, I gotta go and check on Leah. If you're starving, you can go ahead and eat, and I'll warm mine up. She needs me," Rhap explained.

"I understand baby. Take your time," Swerve told her and gave her a kiss.

Rhapsodee made her way to her cousin's condo and let herself in. The only thing Rhap could think of was that Leah must have lost the baby or something. Even though she was still in denial, Rhap knew that Leah would love to have a little mini her running around. It wasn't even five minutes later, Rhap heard the doorknob twisting and her cousin walked in. She instantly got up, walked to the foyer, pulling her in for a hug. Leah broke down crying and Rhap started crying with her cousin.

"What's wrong babe?" Rhap asked after a few minutes.

"I fucked it up with E-Love. Can you believe the man that I started dating, Sebastian, is his dad? I feel like shit. He hates me and he won't hear shit I got to say. Then this pregnancy shit got me crying. I ain't got time to be crying over no nigga," Leah sobbed.

"His dad? Damn, this is bad. Did you, umm, did you..."

"No, I didn't sleep with him, but he not gon' believe that shit. I thought him, and his daddy were 'bout to fight."

"Just give him time to calm down and I'm sure y'all will be fine," Rhap hoped.

"I can't keep this baby now. It's too much. He'll swear I tried to trap him or some shit."

"Leah, I know I should be the last person to judge, but I think you're overthinking and overreacting. Out of the two of us, you always wanted kids. Don't let this situation make you think irrationally. I think you should go to the doctor and see how far along you are. I'll go with you," Rhap suggested.

"Ugh. Why that fine ass man had to be his daddy?" Leah signed.

"Has Sebastian tried to call you since you left?" Rhap sighed.

"So many times, I didn't answer though," Leah shrugged. "I had a few other unknown numbers call me too, but I didn't answer. I clicked with his mom and sister instantly. I know they hate my ass now too," Leah continued.

"You don't know that. Women are more understanding than men, but let's not even worry about that right now. Have you fed my little niece?"

"That's another thing. All this shit happened right before it was time to eat. I stopped and got some McDonald's, but I ended up throwing that shit up. That was my first time even throwing up since I been pregnant."

"Well Swerve cooked. Come over and eat or I'll bring you a plate back," Rhap offered.

"Swerve might be tryna poison yo ass, so I'll pass," Leah replied with a straight face.

"Girl shut up. Believe it or not, we're actually good right now," Rhap confessed.

"Well at least somebody is."

Rhap ended up going to get Leah a plate from her place. Swerve left her a note saying that he was running out to pick up some work boots, and Rhap went back and kept her cousin company for the next three, almost four hours.

*****

On Monday, Rhap was able to schedule Leah her first prenatal appointment for ten o'clock since they had a cancellation. They were told to arrive early to update paperwork, so at a quarter to ten, Rhap was letting Leah out at the front door and told her that she would be in after she parked. Rhap decided to text Swerve on her way in and surprisingly, he texted right back.

Rhap: What do you want for dinner baby?
Swerve: You (tongue emoji)
Rhap: Your wish is my command!

Rhap made her way inside and found her cousin sitting in the corner, filling out paperwork and rolling her eyes. She understood her frustrations because it seemed as if they made you fill out paperwork, they already had just to pass time. Rhap's phone chimed and that reminded her to put it on silent.

Sharon: I have my appointment today. (excited emoji)
Rhap: You need me to meet you?
Sharon: If you're not busy. I know its last minute so I understand if you can't.
Rhap: Girl what time is the appointment? I told you I had your back.
Sharon: It's at eleven. The clinic you recommended.
Rhap: Okay great, I'll see you there!

Leah was sitting back down in her seat right when Rhap was wrapping up her conversation with Sharon.

"That was Sharon. Her appointment is today. I told her I'll meet her here, but if they are quick like they normally are, I'll be able to take you home and come back," Rhap explained.

"You ain't gotta do all that. I can run to Old Navy or somewhere while you here and then we can go eat at Red Lobster. I can just taste their biscuits right now," Leah suggested.

"Sounds even better."

Moments later, Leah's name was called and Rhap followed her to the back. Leah was instructed to give a urine sample and get her vitals checked, so Rhap went and had a seat in the smaller waiting room. That process was pretty fast, but it took longer than expected to get a sonogram because she was already there, so that meant she would still be able to be there for Sharon. A few minutes later, the heartbeat of the baby sounded throughout the room, and it was the sweetest thing that Rhap had ever heard. She could tell that her cousin was in awe as she laid there and listened. It was confirmed that she was eight weeks, and her due date was December 8th.

"Your due date is your birthday girl!" Rhap exclaimed.

"Crazzzzyyy, ain't it?"

The rest of the appointment went well. The nurse handed Leah some sonograms, and Rhap could tell that her cousin was going to go through with the pregnancy. She was happy for her and couldn't wait to start shopping. They made their way out and Leah scheduled her next appointment. Rhap checked her phone and saw that Sharon had texted and told her never mind about the appointment because she had tracked her baby daddy down. Rhap shrugged and headed towards the exit, but before they reached the door, in walked Sharon. Rhap just knew her eyes were playing tricks on her when she looked past her friend and saw her husband.

Von Wiley Hall

Chapter Twenty-Eight

"Oh shit! What the fuck?" Swerve cursed to himself and was stuck on one spot when he saw Rhap and Leah right in front of Sharon at the entrance.

He stood there not knowing what the fuck to do. His mind began racing, trying his best to come up with a logical explanation. Swerve decided that the only thing that he could really do was something that he rarely did, tell the damn truth. Instead of letting Rhap come to him, he slowly made his way over to her so that he could clear his name.

"Hey baby," he smiled.

"What the fuck? Sharon, you mean to tell me that my husband is your baby daddy?" Rhap was livid.

"Rhap, I hate that you had to find out like this," Sharon started saying, but Rhap cut her off by punching her in the mouth.

"Wait Rhap!" Leah grabbed her cousin and Swerve heard her telling Rhap that she couldn't hit a pregnant bitch.

"Swerve you fucked her?" Rhap asked him as tears formed in her eyes.

"No baby. I swear to God! I was tryna clear this shit up and figure out what this bitches angle is. I've done a lot of shit, but this ain't it baby. You gotta believe me," he pleaded.

"I can't believe you hit me when your husband is the one who can't hold his liquor. You need to be checking his ass and not me," Sharon argued while holding her mouth.

"Bitch you got me so fucked up!" Rhap fought to get away from Leah and Swerve was forced to grab her too.

"Is everything okay out here?" a nurse came out and inquired.

"Hell, naw but it's all good. I had an appointment at eleven, but you can cancel it," Sharon said and walked away.

"What the fuck? Hell naw!! Bring yo trifling ass back here so we can get this shit straightened out once and for all," Swerve demanded.

"You better go bitch before I forget that you're pregnant. And as for your lying ass, I've had enough of your bullshit Swerve. Leah let's go eat," Rhap said and walked away, not trying to hear a single word coming from his lying mouth.

"Wait baby, please. Wait let me explain please! I swear that bitch is foul, and I was tryna prove it. You see how she just ran off?" Swerve called out to Rhap, but her and Leah got in the car and left.

The way that Sharon ran off confirmed to Swerve that she wasn't really pregnant. Swerve hopped in his car and followed his wife. She was a few cars ahead of him, but he saw her turning into Ryan's. He got through the light, and he pulled up right beside her car. The two of them must have been in deep conversation because they hadn't gotten out of the car yet. Swerve took that opportunity to get out and go around to Rhap's door. He fully expected her to push it open and hit his ass, but she didn't budge.

"Please hear me out. The day that you caught me and Yoshi, I went to the bar. That lady was the bartender. I got drunk as hell and I woke up at her house on the couch. I didn't see or hear from her anymore until the night that you had her at the house. She claims she has some video of us fucking, but the video she showed me just looks like she's on top of me. Rhap, baby, I swear to God I don't know shit about that girl, and I think she's lying. Why else would she leave the appointment like that?" Swerve poured his heart out.

Swerve heard Leah saying something, but he couldn't make out what it was. Rhap pushed the door open and hit him.

"Swerve, even if that is true, why the fuck wouldn't you tell me? You should have spoken up because you owed me your loyalty not her. You left for work this morning, but I catch you at the clinic with a bitch that's supposed to be my friend. You watched me be her friend and had her kiki'ing and shit in my face, knowing the shit was fake. You just as fake as she is. You got any more secrets? You might as well go ahead and clear the air right now," Rhap cocked her head to the side.

Swerve swallowed the lump that was in his throat. It would be the ideal time to let her know about Yoshi, but there was no fucking way that he could do that.

"Baby no. I just thought I could fix this and not even have to bring it up. We been going through enough."

"Well, well, well, this loser still putting you through it? I told you, I'm still waiting beautiful," a man walked by and said. It was evident that he was talking to Rhap.

"Who the fuck you talking to?" Swerve walked towards him.

"Patna, this ain't what you want," a guy beside the man stepped in and promised.

"Oh, so he can talk shit to my wife, but you gotta talk for him when I step to him?"

"I got it man. My nigga, you a lame ass bitch. I was talking to my future wife over there, but since you got so much air in ya chest, what's up?" the dude challenged Swerve.

All the courage that Swerve had moments ago disappeared. He didn't consider himself a punk, but he was a lover, not a fighter. He took a step back and decided to address Rhap.

"That's what the fuck I thought," the man based and walked away.

"Who the fuck is that Rhap? You are accusing me of shit and this man claiming you as his wife and shit. What the fuck?"

Instead of responding to him, Rhap and Leah both walked around him, going inside of the restaurant. Swerve was livid. He didn't want to go inside and make a scene, but he had something for Rhap's ass.

Von Wiley Hall

124

Chapter Twenty-Nine

As soon as Leah and Rhap were seated, their waitress arrived, and they ordered a lemonade. Since they already knew what they wanted to eat, they went ahead and put their food orders in. Five minutes and two biscuits later, Leah was ready to talk.

"You know I can't stand yo whack ass husband, but I actually believe his dumb ass this time. I been telling you about that bitch Sharon. I gotta put my ears to the streets and get the real deal on that hoe. If she really ain't pregnant, you gotta whoop her ass on GP," Leah said.

"Even if he is telling the truth, he coulda been told me that shit. I'm just tired of being nice. Swerve is taking my kindness for weakness. I'm ready to say fuck them vows, for real for real," Rhap expressed.

"I've never considered you to be weak. You just have a good ass heart, and you love hard. Swerve knows that shit too. Only YOU know how much you can take Rhap. I know I talk a lot of shit, but you gotta do what's best for you. If you gotta leave his ass to make him get his act right, do it. If you gotta leave him for good, do it. It ain't like you can't get a new man. Oh, which reminds me. Who was that fine ass man and where he at? He came in here. We're keeping secrets now? Because I don't recall ever hearing about him."

"Girl, I met that man at Wal-Mart a couple of months ago. He was bold and a tad bit rude as hell, but the shit turned me on," Rhap whispered the last part.

"He's boss status for sure. You see how he made Swerve's ass bitch up. He must be passing through because E-Love got these streets on lock."

"Speaking of E-Love, have you heard from him yet?" Rhap quizzed.

"No, I'm over it. It is what it is," Leah shrugged.

"Whatever," Rhap rolled her eyes.

Before Leah could reply, the mystery man took a seat beside Rhap and the other guy sat beside her. She could have sworn that she saw a smile on her cousin's face and that shocked the shit out of her, but Leah could understand why. The man was fine as hell.

"Ummm, excuse y'all?" Leah questioned.

"I'm Black. That's my cousin, Sosa. I know the name of my future wife, Rhapsodee. What's yours?"

"You are bold as hell just like my cousin said," Leah said and took a sip of her drink.

"I told you, the nigga called my ring a crackerjack box ring."

Leah noticed the way that her cousin was looking back at him. If one didn't know any better, you would swear that the two of them had been together for years.

"So, what's your name, miss lady?" Sosa asked.

"It's Leah, and I don't mean to be rude, but I'm not interested. I'm sorry," Leah told him.

"Well at least you're honest and straightforward, and you're beautiful, but I'll back off," Sosa replied.

"Well I just need y'all to be cordial because I need to spend some time with my baby right here," Black affirmed.

Black reminded Leah of E-Love, and it slick put her in her feelings. Just as quick as she got in them, she got out of them when the waitress appeared and sat their food down in front of them. She took a bite of her cubed steak and it was delicious. Leah wanted to ask for a piece of Rhap's grilled pork chop but didn't want to look greedy in front of their uninvited guests. Black started a conversation and the four of them all conversed as if they were old friends. Leah really didn't mind because she needed the distraction. Sosa was still cool even though she shot him down early on. Most men acted like bitches if you rejected them, but he acted as if nothing happened.

When the lady brought the tickets, Black grabbed them and paid for everyone's food. Leah excused herself to go to the bathroom, but she heard Black asking Rhap for her number. She made her way inside and relieved her bladder. After washing her hands, Leah adjusted her braids and made a mental note to call her cousin for a touch up. She was ready to take her hair down. There had been times where she had gone a whole year with braids, and it was looking like 2020 was going to be one of those years. After drying her hands,

Hard and Ruthless

Leah exited the bathroom and felt a bump once she rounded the corner. She looked up and couldn't believe her eyes. It had been years since Leah had laid eyes on the man who had taken her virginity.

Von Wiley Hall

Chapter Thirty

Ever since finding out that his girl had been involved with his dad, E-Love had been closed up in the hotel room drinking. It was going on seventy-two hours and he had yet to talk to anyone, after the incident when his dick went limp. He was normally the type who didn't let shit bother him so bad to the point of shutting everyone out, so he knew his family was worried, especially his mom. E-Love figured his mother would be understanding of how he felt, so he decided that he needed to head home. Plus, he needed to take another shower, put on some fresh clothes and return her car before she put a hit out on his ass.

E-Love pulled up to his mom's house fifteen minutes after he left the hotel. As soon as he made it in the house, his mom was standing there with her hands on her hips looking like she was ready to fuck him up.

"Sorry mom."

"That's all you got to say?"

"I have to shower and change clothes. I'll be back."

He heard his mom mumble something, but E-Love kept going. After taking a hot shower, E-Love threw on a white tee and some Khaki shorts. His selection of clothing at his mom's crib wasn't all that great, but it would do. The shower refreshed him, and he knew that he needed to get back to handling his business. Bobby B was probably ready to kick his ass, but he needed the mental break, so his homie would have to understand.

"Ma, I need to use your old car to get to the crib," E-Love said when he entered the living room.

"If you wouldn't have been acting so damn stupid, you coulda left the same way you came."

E-Love just knew that his ears were playing tricks on him. Wasn't no way in hell his mom was defending Leah. He just couldn't believe that shit and apparently his facial expression showed it.

"Yeah I said it. E-Love. I just met that girl, and I can tell that she's a good one. Now you know I know you better than you know your damn self, and I'm sure you done put her through hell, but she still with your ass. All I'm saying is you need to at least hear her out. The damn girl didn't even sleep with your daddy. They only went on a few dates."

"So, she told you that and you believed her after meeting her once?"

"No. She didn't talk to any of us, but your dad did. I believe him. He has no reason to lie. She probably saw some of you in your dad, think about it that way," his mother explained.

"Mom, with all due respect. If she has anything to do with my dad, especially while being with me, it's over. Now, can I use your old car or what? I got some business to take care of."

'Okay Eric. Be stubborn if you want to. Just know that when you leave those streets, it ain't nothing like having a real one to come home to," she said and tossed him the keys.

"I hear ya Ma. I love you" he kissed her on the cheek and left.

When E-Love got in the car, he plugged his phone in the charger that was already in there. His battery was dead, so he had to wait a few minutes for it to get a little juice before powering it on. E-Love stopped and gassed up and was on 285 heading north within fifteen minutes. He sent a text to his homie Bobby B so that he could give him a brief rundown on everything before they even met up. The shit was embarrassing for him to talk about. *It is what it is* E-Love thought as he placed the call.

Chapter Thirty-One

Rhap couldn't believe the feelings that she was experiencing. Seeing Black again only brought back memories of their very first encounter. She knew that she shouldn't have been feeling that way, but with everything that Swerve had put her through, she was ready to let her hair down and say fuck it. Leah was gone to the bathroom longer than normal and Rhap was starting to worry.

"Your cousin is a big girl. I need you to focus on me for now," Black commanded

"Focus on you huh? I think I'll get myself in trouble if I do that," Rhap chuckled.

"You a grown ass woman. Ain't no such thing as getting in trouble. I'm still waiting on you to give me your number. I'm not gon' ask again. And before you try to cop a fake attitude, I'm just gon' take it," Black reached over and grabbed her phone.

Swerve called as he picked it up and he declined the call. Surprisingly, Rhap didn't even care. Black grabbed her and put her thumb on the home button, unlocking her phone. She saw him dialing a number and knew that he had to be calling himself. She had already made up her mind that she was going to give him her number, but he made it that much easier.

"Yeah I know you wanted me to have it, so I just helped us both out," he told her, sitting her phone back down.

"You think you know me or something?"

"Not completely, but in time I will. So, are we counting this shit as our first date or when you wanna make it happen?"

"You're so damn cocky!"

'Confident baby, I'm confident. Never cocky," he swooned.

"I like that. Mr. Confident. So, tell me what it is that you're looking for because you clearly know I'm a married woman."

"To start, I just wanna take it slow. I'ma give you time to end that shit you got goin' on, you deserve better and better is me. That nigga left you alone with a man that called you his future wife. If you ask me, that's a bitch. You're the most beautiful woman I've ever seen, and I've thought about you countless times since the day at Wal-Mart. I told myself if I ever saw you again, you would be mine. I could have looked you up and all that other shit, but I wanted it to happen naturally. Now, how much time do you need?"

Rhapsodee was speechless after Black finished talking. Thankfully, Leah walked up to the table just in time because her words were caught in her throat.

"Rhap, I'm gonna get dropped off at home. You gon' be okay?"

"Yeah, I'll text you," Rhap replied and disappeared.

"Since you free, let's get outta here. Sosa you…"

"I'm two steps ahead of ya boss. I'll meet you at the spot later."

An hour later, Rhap and Black were out at the reservoir, taking in the beauty. It was a lovely April day and Rhap was glad they weren't getting any April showers. Swerve called a few more times, but Rhap ended up powering her phone off to limit the distractions. She felt so carefree and enjoyed every second with Black. She knew that she would have to deal with her husband later, but later it would be and not at that moment.

"I haven't asked this, but I've learned not to assume so let me ask anyway…are you single? If so, why?"

"I knew it was coming. Yeah, I'm single, but you do know a man got needs. One thing about me, I'm always honest, so it's up to the other person on whether or not they can deal with it, but once I see any sign that they can't, I'm done. I got too much to lose to deal with drama and bullshit," Black explained.

'Hmph."

"Humph? That's all you got to say?"

"I didn't mean it like that. You're being honest, so I gotta respect it. What do you do?"

"Let's just say I'm a jack of all trades," he coolly replied.

"Being honest huh?"

"Yep. Sometimes, the less you know the better. I'm guessing you're a nurse since you had on scrubs the first time I saw you. Where you work?"

"Yes, I'm a nurse. A traveling nurse actually. When you saw me, I was just getting back into town. I came home early to surprise my husband, but I was the one who got surprised," Rhap reminisced.

"What did that fuck nigga do?" Black based.

Rhap thought for a second on whether or not she wanted to discuss her marital problems with Black. When he put his arm around her, she felt at ease and comfortable with him that she broke down her whole damn relationship. He listened to her and when she finished, he gave her advice from a man's point of view. Black still considered Swerve to be a bitch ass nigga, but he told her that he respected her that even more for trying to make it work. Before Rhap knew it, it was almost four o'clock and she remembered Black saying that he had a meeting to go to.

"Didn't you have somewhere to be?"

"My partner texted and said that he was running a lil late. You ready to get rid of me or something?"

"Oh no. I'm enjoying the moment. I think I've walked up an appetite though. I'm still undecided on whether or not I wanna go home and cook or just grab myself something?"

"How bout we go get something together and then I'll let you go?" Black suggested.

Rhap agreed and they ended up at Chick-Fil-A because she wanted a chicken sandwich. Before they ended their impromptu day together, Rhap agreed to see Black again the next day before he left town. She expected him to give her a kiss before they parted ways, but the firm hug he gave her was enough to hold her over. She powered her phone on and talked to him until she arrived at her place.

"I really enjoyed you today. Although I know it was wrong, it was just what I needed."

"You ain't seen nothing yet Miss Rhapsodee. You ain't seen nothing yet. I'll call you tomorrow beautiful."

"I look forward to it, handsome."

Rhap ended the call and dreaded going inside, but she knew that she had to get it over with. She had made it up in her mind that she was going to tell Swerve that she felt like the marriage had run its course. After talking to Black all day, it gave Rhap a brand-new perspective on life. When he told her that holding on to a dead situation out of guilt or putting someone else's feelings first was a sure way for a lifetime of unhappiness, she felt that shit. After sitting there for a few more minutes basking in her thoughts from the day, Rhap finally got out of the car. Before she made it to the door, she searched her purse and grabbed her keys. When she was about to insert her key, the door opened, and Swerve stood there reeking of alcohol.

"So, you just said fuck me and ignored all my calls and texts huh? Bitch you think you gone play me and get away with it?" he barked.

"Bitch? Nigga you better watch how the fuck you talk to me. I ain't gonna be nan nother bitch. Believe that! But after all that shit you have put me through, nigga please. Now more Swerve! I don't have time for your ship," Rhap stepped around and made her way in.

As soon as the door closed, Swerve grabbed her and spun her around. Before she could say anything else, he hit Rhapsodee in the face so hard that all she could do was fall to the floor and scream. He covered her mouth and began beating the fuck out of her. All the fight left her body and all she saw was black.

Chapter Thirty-Two

When Swerve left the restaurant, he was enraged. If he wasn't scared of going to jail or getting his ass beat, he would have gone head to head with that big nigga. He drove straight to the liquor store and purchased some vodka. Swerve thought about driving out to Yoshi's, but he wasn't in the best mood and didn't want to take his frustrations out on her. He went home and began drinking. When Swerve laid back on the couch, him and Rhap's wedding album caught his eye. He leaned forward and grabbed it, turning the pages. Even though Swerve knew he had fucked up before, that was really a happy day. If he had to rewind, he would do it all over again.

The more he turned the pages, his mood changed. Swerve knew that Rhap would never do him dirty, but what the dude said continued to weigh heavy on his mind. He picked up his phone and called her, but it rang once and went to voicemail. Swerve threw his phone down and started back drinking. After calling Rap's phone several times, all to no avail, Swerve's mind began to wander. He wanted to go back to the restaurant, but he didn't want to run into the same guy again. He laid back and continued drinking. Once the bottle was gone, Swerve passed out on the couch.

It was dark outside when Swerve woke up and had a banging headache. Thoughts from the day popped back into his mind. He hopped up to see of Rhapsodee had made it home. Swerve went to the kitchen and downed the Peach Cîroc that Rhap had in the cabinet. He walked to the door with the intent on going to find his wife, but when he opened it, there she was. Letting the alcohol fuel his rage and after beating Rhap to a bloody pulp, Swerve dropped down beside her and started crying.

"Look what you made me do. I'm sorry baby. I'm so sorry," he sobbed.

Swerve looked up and looked down at Rhapsodee again and she still wasn't moving. He went to the kitchen and filled a pot with water. He walked back to the foyer and threw it on her. Faint moans escaped her lips, and he knew that she wasn't dead. There was no way that he could take her to the hospital without incriminating himself, so he tossed that idea out of his mind. Swerve paced the floor trying to figure out his next move.

"Think...fuck...think Swerve think," he continued pacing the floor & hitting himself.

After a few minutes, Swerve picked Rhapsodee up and carried her to the bedroom. She tried to fight him with the little strength that she had, but one more hit and she was back out. Swerve tied her to the bed by her hands and feet and covered her mouth.

"When I get back, we gonna talk about how to fix this marriage that you fucked up!" Swerve spat and left. He didn't have a particular destination in mind when he left home but ended up at Yoshi's. Swerved used his key and let himself in, and then walked into the bedroom and found Yoshi sound asleep. He smiled while thinking about how she was doing all the right things while Rhap was fucking up. She must have felt his presence because she rolled over and then smiled when she locked eyes with him.

"What are you doing here babe? I didn't think I was gonna see you till Monday."

"You never know when I might pop up. I know you been dealing with a lot, so tonight it's all about you. I gotta leave early, but we got all night," said Swerve.

Yoshi didn't waste any time. As soon as he slipped out of his clothes, her mouth was on his dick. All of his stress was gone for the rest of the night, but he knew the next morning, it would be back.

It was fifteen minutes after nine when Swerve made it home. He could hear soft cries coming from Rhap before he reached the bedroom. Her hands and feet were tied tight as hell, so he knew she had to be in place, and she was. Swerve flicked the light on and walked over to the bed. He had no idea that he had did that much damage to his wife. Tears threatened to fall from his eyes, but he blinked them back. Rhap lay there with two black eyes and he saw bruises on her neck also.

Swerve was sure that she had more damage, but he didn't have the courage to check.

Hard and Ruthless

"You made me do this baby. Now, I am sorry I had to, but you disrespected our vows. You said you was with me til death us part. Are you ready to die?" Swerve asked.

Rhap didn't answer, tears ran freely down her face. He gave her a few seconds to answer, but she never did. Swerve too that moment to go into the closet and retrieve his Smith and Wesson.

"I asked you a question. Are you ready to die?"

She frantically shook her head no and Swerve was pleased with her answer.

"If you try anything stupid, I will kill you. I'm not 'bout to watch over you twenty-four seven either. Do I have to?" he cocked his head to the side.

She shook her head once again and Swerve sat down on the bed beside her. "I want our marriage to work. I'll set up our next counseling session for two weeks. I'm 'bout to find you something to eat, and I'll give you some pain meds. I'll uncover your mouth, but if you scream, you gone get a repeat of last night."

He removed the bandana from her mouth and then went into the kitchen and fixed Rhapsodee some cereal and a glass of orange juice. After grabbing the Tylenol, Swerve went back into the bedroom and fed Rhap and then gave her pain meds. He didn't know what the fuck his next move was going to be, but he knew he wasn't about the lose his wife.

Von Wiley Hall

Chapter Thirty-Three

Black hadn't run across a woman like Rhapsodee in a long ass time. The more he thought about it, he didn't know if he ever had. Running unto her again had made his day and Black looked forward to the next day. He was a man that had his shit together. The only thing was missing was a queen. Rhapsodee was the queen that was going to complete his throne. Soon, he would be stepping down completely from his positions and ready to reap the benefits of his hard labor. Black agreed to give Rhapsodee some time to get her shit together, but the more he thought about it, he knew that he wasn't going to have much patience.

A call came through on Blacks phone and he answered when he sat that it was Sosa.

"What up?"

"You done caking Romeo?" Sosa laughed.

"Nigga shut the fuck up! Y'all ready?"

"Yeah we already at the spot. You on the way?

"Be there in five," Black confirmed and ended the call.

Right on time, Black pulled up to the meeting location and parked. Black always made it a habit to pay attention to every damn thang including the vehicles that people drove and there was one that he didn't recognize. He made his way back inside and his homie greeted him at the door.

"Whose Toyota is that outside?"

"Oh, that's my OG's old car. I had to drive it back after some bullshit popped off, but I'll tell ya 'bout that after we talk about this business," E-Love told him.

"Aww shit. That look tells me this 'bout to be some of that good bullshit. I gotta tell you some shit too, but it's good on my end though," Black laughed.

"At least one of us got some good news, but let's talk about the business first," E-Love motioned.

Black filled the crew in on what happened after the meeting in Birmingham. He let them know that he took care of that bitch nigga that set the meeting up and one of the passengers, but the driver of the car was still on the loose. They discussed the expansion plan and Black also hinted at his retirement. The thought of dying in the street like his dad was a painful thought. E-Love and Black's fathers were street legends in Biloxi, Mississippi, and they groomed their sons to take over the entire south. Black had several territories in Texas on lock. They had a pretty solid team behind them, but every now and then, there was that one that fucked up. E-Love's homie being the most recent. The business meeting was over and everyone except Black, E-Love Sosa and Bobby B were gone. Black had a good feeling about the direction in which they were heading.

"What do you got to drink in this muthafucka? Black asked.

Bobby got up and came back with a bottle of Henny and a bottle of Crown. The four men poured themselves a drink and then sat down so the shit talking session could begin. Black noticed the stressed look on his homie's face, and he hoped the shit wasn't as bad as E-Love was making it out to be. Blacked downed his drink and downed another one and said "damn" because it must be some bad shot for real.

"My girl fuckin' around with my dad," E-Love finally blurted out.

"What the fuck/' Sosa yelled.

"Dammmnnn!" Black said.

"I still think it gotta be more to the story," Bobby B chimed in.

"Wait, wait, wait. Let's back up first. Your girl? When the fuck you start claiming a girl?" Black wanted to know.

"I was waiting on you to ask that," Bobby B laughed.

"Nigga, backup and start from the beginning," Black requested.

"Look niggas, Leah. I'm in love with Leah, the girl I been kicking it wit. We made shit official and then I took her to meet my folks. I grabbed her phone to call pops and she got this niggas number saved as some got damn Mr. Irresistible. Ain't shit else I need to hear. Moms ain't even on my side, so at least my damn boys will see my point of view," E-Love explained.

'She fucked pops?" Black asked, trying to get clarification.

"Here you go! Man, I don't know, but does it really matter?' E-Love shrugged.

"I mean, yeah. That is like if I meet a girl, but I can tell she ain't for me, I ain't gon' get mad if Sosa get at her.

"Well the name Leah is off my list of women now. The way this black beauty named Leah just shut my ass down, fuck all the Leah's!" Sosa said.

"Black beauty? Nigga did you try to push up on my girl?" E-love stood up.

"Aww hell. It can't be the same Leah. She was with my future wife. Her name is Rhapsodee," Black stood up to keep E-Love from doing anything crazy.

"This a small ass world. It's his Leah!" E-Love laughed.

"Well shit. Can you blame your Pops for tryna holla?" Sosa queried.

"Nigga!! Don't make me..."

"E-Love, we all boys here. Let's talk about this shit aight?" Black reasoned.

"Now my news was about Rhapsodee, but I damn shol' didn't know you was gon' know 'em. The Leah chick, she seems like a real one man. I think you need to put your pride to the side and talk to pops and then go get ya girl," Black stated.

E-Love sat there looking like he had lost his best friend when Bobby B chimed in.

"I told that nigga that. He been on one since he's been back. He can't even function without that damn girl. She's definitely a real one. Better snatch her up before someone else does."

The four of them drank and talked shit for the next couple of hours. Afterwards Black went to the apartment he owned in Candy-land and crashed. He was looking forward to seeing Rhapsodee before he had to hit the road.

*****

The next morning, Black rolled over and the first thing he did was send Rhap a text. He didn't expect her to reply back instantly, considering her situation, so he sat the phone down and got up so that he could get his day started. He went to the kitchen and fixed a bowl of Raisin Bran. If it wasn't for the maid service he had on payroll, there wouldn't ever be anything to eat at his place because he was barely there. After eating two bowls of cereal, Black had his morning blunt and then hopped into the shower. When he got out, he picked up his phone and saw that it was twenty minutes after eleven and Rhap still hadn't replied. He was really expecting a reply by then, so he sent another text, threw the phone down, and then started getting dressed.

Thirty minutes later, Black was dressed casually in a yellow Polo shirt, Khaki's and some brown Polo slides. His phone chimed and he knew that it had to be Rhap. He was ready to spoil her a little bit and show her how a real nigga treated his queen.

My Queen: Giving you my number was the worst mistake I ever made. I love my husband and I can't talk to you anymore.

"What the fuck she on?" Black mumbled to himself.

Black: Oh, it's like that?

My Queen: Straight like that, I don't know what I saw in yo fake thug ass anyway. Fuck off before my husband finds you and beats yo ass!!

Black stood there in total disbelief. He thought that maybe it could have been that bitch as nigga texting from Rhap's phone, but she had a lock code on it, so he threw that option out. Feeling played like a muthafucka, Black grabbed his phone, his keys and shit and sent Sosa a text, letting him know that he was ready to roll! There wasn't shit else for him where he was at the moment.

"Ain't this bout a bitch," Black fumed and left.

*****

Sharon stared at the fifteen pregnancy tests and got pissed the fuck off. She didn't really sleep with Swerve because the nigga wouldn't get hard in his sleep. She blamed that in the shit she has slipped in his drink. When Swerve walked into Dudley's that night, Sharon was on cloud nine. She felt like she wasn't going to ever see him again, and she couldn't let that opportunity pass her by. After she befriended Rhapsodee and found out Swerve was her husband, being a true friend went straight out of the window because Sharon wanted revenge for how Swerve had made her feel like shit. Sharon remembered that night like it was yesterday.

*****

Club Palladium was packed, and Sharon was racking up on tips. Even though this was her second part-time job, she was doing good. The big money was in the private rooms and she couldn't wait to be solicited! She was growing impatient, but shortly after, a high yellow nigga with waves was giving her the eye. That was all Sharon needed to see to make her head in his direction. Not even ten minutes later, they were in a private room and Sharon was giving Swerve the best head he ever had in his life. She knew that because he told her and told her that he loved her when she has his dick and balls in her throat. It had to be his first time in the private room because the nigga didn't even have a condom, but that didn't stop from letting Sharon ride the shit out of him.

She felt a strong ass connection with him. It was something that she had never felt before. When Sharon looked at his ring finger, there was no ring, but she saw a print. She figured he must have been recently divorced, or he had just taken it off. She hoped he was recently divorced because the way they fucked each other, she had decided that she wasn't going to let him get away. He had given her his full name while fucking. She chucked it up to the power of the pussy.

"Damn baby. Ain't nobody ever made me cum like that before." Sharon giggled after she washed off and then washed her new light skinned boo off.

"That shit was the bomb," he replied.

"You wanna meet up for breakfast?" she cooed.

"Breakfast? Like out in public?" Swerve asked.

Sharon was taken aback by his reply but figured she must have been taking it the wrong way.

"Ummm, yeah, unless you want me to cook for you? But I was thinking we could do Waffle House?" She suggested.

Sean burst out laughing and Sharon was instantly pissed.

"What's so fucking funny?"

"I just fucked you in this private room for the first time I met you. Do you honestly think I would go out with you? Or even take you seriously for that matter? You stripper bitches gotta be the dumbest broads on planet Earth," he laughed hysterically.

"I know the fuck you just didn't say that to me," She fumed.

"I know the fuck I did. The only thing you can do for me is fuck me in this room, bitch. I got a whole wife at home anyway. This was just some stripper pussy. I came here because she'll never find out about it. Didn't think yo ass was gon' fall in love," he continued to laugh and belittle her.

Sharon knew he didn't recognize her because of her long weave, fake lashes and makeup.

Sharon wanted to cry, but she wasn't going to give him the satisfaction. She began seeing red. All while he got dressed, he continued talking shit and Sharon vowed right then and there to make his life a living hell.

*****

The ringing of Sharon's phone broke her from her reverie. She saw that it was one of her coworkers calling and ignored it. Sharon had to go back to the drawing board to figure out how she could fuck Swerve's life up and also Rhap for punching her ass.

Chapter Thirty-Four

It had been two weeks since the incident with E-Love, and it was two weeks before Leah was scheduled to leave and go visit with her parents and she couldn't wait. That alone made her smile. Leah couldn't lie and say that she didn't miss E-Love, but Woody had been keeping her company. Woody was her first love and they really didn't have a bad breakup. It was one of those situations where he wanted to leave after high school and Leah chose to stay in the area. If she wanted to leave, she would have left with her parents, but she loved Atlanta. As long as she could travel whenever she wanted to, she was cool with the city life. The last she heard, Woody was married with kids and living the quote unquote "good life." It was a pleasant surprise to see him and quite shocking to find out that he was back in Atlanta, maybe for good, depending on whether or not he accepted the job offer at a local news station.

Leah had just hung up with him. He was being very persistent, but she had to decline his lunch offer. She really wasn't trying to jump into anything new and she was honest with him about that. But it felt good to have someone to talk to, especially since her cousin has been acting strange. Leah had vented all she could to Twin also but getting a man's point of view on her drama was much needed and it confirmed that she really didn't do anything wrong. Leah picked her phone back up and placed a FaceTime call to Rhap. She didn't answer, but she called back the regular way in less than thirty seconds.

"You can't answer FaceTime calls now? Every time I made one, you ignored it and called back regular or text. What's wrong with you?" Leah fussed.

"Nothing is wrong Leah. I'm at work and…"

"Being at work ain't never stopped us from talking on FaceTime. I haven't seen you since that day at the restaurant, and I'm getting sick of your excuses. Where are you working at? I'm coming to see you." Leah cut her off.

"No. I'm fine, but I'm too far away. I'll be home soon. I went ahead and left the next day. I had to…I just had to leave for this assignment right away," Rhap explained. Her and Swerve were in Florida. They took a flight there after he returned the next morning after beating her. It was his way of keeping people from popping up at their condo and seeing what was really going on.

Leah felt like something wasn't right, but she couldn't prove it. Her cousin didn't even sound like herself. For the past two weeks, Rhap had been pretty much avoiding her.

'What did Swerve do to you?"

"What? Huh?"

"Don't what, huh me. Something ain't right. I can just feel it!"

"Girl, you still crazy. I got a patient buzzing me, so I'ma call you back. I love you girl, bye." Rhap hung up before she could reply.

"What the fuck?" Leah fumed to herself.

Before she could call back, a text from Twin came through.

When Leah clicked on the message icon, she noticed that it was actually a live video that had been screen recorded, Leah paused it and put her headphones in, so she could turned the volume all the way up. No one ever really barged into her office, but she liked to be precautious anyway. Leah's blood began to boil as she listened to Sharon on Instagram live spilling tea about everything that she had been doing to fuck a dog ass nigga's life up. She even went into details about how the nigga played her and why she wanted revenge. None of them followed the bitch on Instagram, but they had a fake page that they shared to lurk, and Twin had hit the jackpot with a live video. Sharon accepted them, not knowing who the hell they were, and it paid off.

Sharon was drunk as hell in that video. It was an hour and ten minutes long, and Leah watched every second of it. As if on cue, Twin was calling as soon as it ended.

"I timed it. I know you done. That shit is crazy! You were right, you was right. Poor Rhap. I feel so bad for her. She is doing everything to save her marriage while he outchea passing out the dick like he the ice cream man or somethin'. I don't wanna send that in a group chat, but I think you should talk to her about it," Twin rambled on and on.

"That low down, dirty stankin' ass bitch. I knew it. I knew it, Twin. Swerve's dog ass was telling the truth about not sleeping with her then. Yhat's why he didn't remember fuckin' her before huh?" Leah replied.

Her and Twin talked for over an hour analyzing the entire situation and trying to come up with the best solution.

"I'm finna go find that bitch and beat her ass myself. Rhap can get her later!" Leah fumed.

"Wait, wait! You pregnant or did you forget? You can't be fighting, trick. Ain't 'bout to have my baby stressed the fuck out and coming out looking like E.T," Twin intervened.

"Hush. You're so damn stupid! Damn, but I really be forgetting that shit," Leah laughed at Twin and rubbed her belly.

"Well I ain't gon' forget. I got my back. You gotta be on your best behavior though. Have you had a real conversation with Rhap yet?"

"No, and her ass hung up on me earlier. I'm finna just gon' and call her back now. She said she's working in Florida. See if you can see what Swerve's been up to. I haven't seen him come home not one day with his dog ass," Leah fussed.

She ended the call with Twin and was about to call Rhap. Before she could dial the number, her mom's picture popped up on the screen.

"Heeyy Ma," Leah smiled

"Leah, you gotta get here," her mom sobbed, and Leah's heart dropped.

"Mom, I'll see you soon," Leah hung up.

She began searching for flights to Tampa. Her parents lived about thirty minutes from the city but flying to any airport that was in close proximity would be fine. She started getting any flights out of Atlanta.

"Uggghhh!! Leah screamed.

She ended up taking a flight out the next morning. It was almost two and it was going to take a little over two hours to get there, but Leah booked the flight anyway. She had a travel bag in the car and that was going to have to do until she could get to some stores down there. Leah texted her assistant and told her that she had a family emergency and would be out of the office for a while. She hopped in her car and could barely function, but she knew that she had to keep it together. Thoughts of calling E-Love flooded her mind, but she had to focus. She didn't want to put her problem on Woody, so she shifted the car into gear and took off. As soon as she bypassed the State Trooper on I-20 east where most of the construction was taking place, she turned on her emergency blinkers and put the pedal to the medal.

*****

God must have been on her side because she found a parking spot in the first parking lot. It didn't even matter the cost. Leah just parked and hopped out and pretty much ran full speed. On the way, she prayed that the ticket agency played nice because she was cutting it super close. They answered her prayers and the announcement for the last call to board her flight was being made right as Leah made it to the correct gate. She boarded the plane and blew out a breath of relief when she finally sat in her seat. The tears that Leah wouldn't allow to fall while she was driving, finally fell freely down her face. Her emotions were all over the place because she knew that something had to be wrong with her dad. She couldn't get the sound of her mom's voice out of her head. Leah felt someone tap her and she opened her eyes, finding one of the flight attendants handing her some Kleenex.

"Thank you," she muffled and wiped her fears away.

Across the aisle, the prettiest little baby was looking at her and smiling. That made Leah's heart melt. She thought about the life that was growing inside of her. She knew that sooner or later she was going to have to tell E-Love. No matter the status of their relationship, he still had a right to know. The normal announcements were made before takeoff, and Leah put her headphones in and ignored them all. She let her music sing to her and two hours later, they were landing. Even though she tried to get a nap, it was impossible because her mind was racing.

Hard and Ruthless

As soon as she got off the plane, Leah called her Mom to find out her exact location. She expected her to be at the hospital or somewhere, but her mom told her that she was at the house. Leah requested an Uber, and one was available right away. It took about thirty minutes, just as expected, to make it out to her parents. Thankfully, Leah kept their house key on her keyring, so she was able to let herself in upon arrival! When she walked inside, the TV was on and Leah saw a nurse heading towards the kitchen.

"Oh hi. You must be Leah," the nurse smiled when Leah got closer.

"I am. Can you tell me what's going on please?" Leah requested.

"Well, I'm not sure I should be the..."

"Michelle?" Leah said after looking at her name tag.

Von Wiley Hall

Chapter Thirty-Five

"My mom called me out of the blue telling me to get here. I walk in and see a nurse. Clearly, they've been keeping secrets and I need to know what I'm walking into. Please tell me what's going on," Leah pleaded.

"Your mom wants to tell you, Sweetie, but I'm with hospice."

Just hearing that made Leah's heart drop. A new batch of tears threatened to fall, but Leah stopped them. She had to go into the room and check on her parents.

"I know you don't know me, but I'm here for you," Michelle expressed.

"Thank you," Leah whispered.

She made her way to her parent's extravagant bedroom and saw her dad lying in the bed, looking helpless. Her mom was right by his side, sitting in a chair, holding his hand. Leah made her way to the bed and grabbed her dad's hand, and he briefly opened his eyes.

"Hey baby girl," he spoke in a low voice.

"Daddy, how are you?"

"I'm sorry for not wanting you to know. Please forgive me."

"Dad, you're gonna be alright. I forgive you. What can I do to help?" she asked as tears streamed down her face.

"Just forgive me and take care of your mom okay. I was holding on for you baby girl! Just know that I love you dearly."

"I love…"

As those words left his mouth and before she could reciprocate her love, he released the grip he had on her hands, and Leah literally felt his breath leave his body. Leah fell over into him sobbing until she couldn't sob anymore. Her mom was crying hysterically also, but she tried her best to comfort her daughter. Leah later found out that her dad was diagnosed with stage four prostate cancer a few months ago and refused chemo. He said that he had lived his life and he was content. Leah knew that she had to get it together and be strong for her mom. After the morgue came and picked up her dad's body, Leah and her mom talked for hours. After Leah kept rubbing her stomach, her mom pretty much guessed that she was pregnant, and Leah confirmed it.

"You be sure you make up with that man. I can hear how much you love him. I don't even wanna know what happened, but I hope you can experience a love as great as me and your father. You know they say grief is the final act. I love that man with all of my heart," her mom confessed.

"I know you do mom. I know you do. I know the thought of living without him is scary, but I'm gonna be here for you."

"I'll be just fine darling. I'm so glad that you got here when you did. I love you baby," her mom smiled.

"I love you too mom." They hugged and then both said goodnight.

The next morning, Leah got up and went into her parent's room after she didn't see her mom in the kitchen. That was very strange because she was always up with the chickens drinking coffee, so Leah went in search of her mom. Finding her still sleeping, Leah walked over to the bed and noticed she wasn't breathing. Instantly, she grabbed her mom's hand, and it was cold as ice.

"Nooo! Nooo! Not you too! Mama! Mama! Daddy! Nooo! Nooo!" Leah cried her heart out, her heart breaking with her new reality. A brand-new fresh set of tears emerged and streamed down her face. She felt like she was suffocating from all the death that suddenly surrounded her and her emotions were running rampant. Leah couldn't believe she was now parentless within hours of each other.

Chapter Thirty-Six

Going hard and building his money was all E-Love knew, and he had been doing a thousand times harder to keep his mind from wandering. As hard as he was going, the shit still wasn't working. Thoughts of Leah stayed on his mind. He wasn't even big on social media, but he had accounts to make sure his workers weren't posting stupid shit, and he was friends with Leah on everything. She hadn't been posting shit, so it made E-Love feel like she must have closed herself out of the world. A lot of duties that E-Love normally delegated to the crew he was doing himself.

He was in the back room at the trap house on Moreland Avenue counting money. It was midway through May, which was pretty much summertime in Atlanta, and the sales had more than tripled. The new product that him and Black had copped was selling like hotcakes. When E-Love was done counting, the total for half the month was three quarters of a million dollars. He was in shock, but happy as fuck. That was the first time he smiled since the cookout. Making money was always good. After putting the money to the side for re-up and splitting everyone's earnings, E-Love locked shit up and left.

It was a little after six when E-Love got in his car. He drove the hell out of his mom's car until her and his sister came and got it the week before. They both tried to lecture him yet again, but he still wasn't hearing the shit. As soon as E-Love drove away, his phone rang, and he saw it was Black.

"What up bruh?"

"Think I finally got the location on that nigga. Thing is, he be in and out, and if the information that this shawty gave me is correct, he'll be back in town at the end of this month," Black explained.

"Word?"

"Yup, so it is on in a couple weeks, but on another note, you done made up with ya girl?"

"Nigga, have you? The way you left here pissed," E-Love diverted the conversation.

"Maannn, forget I brought it up. Bye," Black tried hanging up, but E-Love stopped him,

"Nah, nah, nah, don't try to hang up now," E-love laughed.

Black had told him all about how Rhap played him, It didn't sound like the Rhap he knew, and he tried to tell his boy that, but all Black did was flip the situation on him, so E-Love dropped it.

"Fuck you, nigga. I gotta go," Black hung up and E-Love couldn't do shit but laugh at his ass.

E-Love loved Rhap like a sister, and he would be happy if his bruh would snatch her away from that lame. Never being the hating type, or a nigga to get in other folk business, E-Love knew that Swerve wasn't shit. He lived by the saying what's done in the dark shall come to the light, and he knew sooner or later Rhap would figure shit out. Hell, his brand-new relationship was fucked up, so he wasn't the one to figure out other folks shit anyway. E-Love whipped into Burger King, so that he could grab a whopper. He paid for his food and ignored the cashier that was tryna throw the pussy at him. He couldn't lie and say he didn't need any, but he didn't have time to be dealing with anyone new. E-Love made up his mind that he would hit up one of his old lil thots to meet him at one of his spots. He pulled up at the crib and went inside. All of his fries were gone because he wanted to eat them while they were hot, but he was ready to smash his whopper. Four bites in and his phone rang. E-Love looked at it and threw it down when he saw that it was his dad calling. He finished off the rest of his burger and then saw that his dad left a voicemail. Just that gesture alone made E-Love know that his dad was fed the fuck up. He listened to five seconds of the message and it confirmed he was right. Reluctantly, E-Love stopped listening to the voicemail and just went ahead and called his old man back.

"Eric Langford, don't make me have to break my foot off in yo ass! I've let this fuckin' tantrum of yours go on longer than I should have, but the shit stops now," Sebastian based as he answered his phone.

E-Love knew by that tone that challenging his dad was only going to make it worse, so he bit his tongue.

154

Hard and Ruthless

"Me and that young lady met during Mardi Gras weekend. We went on a couple of dates, but then she told me that the man she loved finally committed to her, so I backed off. I did try to get her to reconsider, but she was adamant. And to answer your unspoken question, we never fucked so get that shit out of your head now, Never in a million years did I expect you to be the man that she was in love with. Just thinking back on how you spoke about your new girl, you two are meant to be together. Stop being so damn stubborn and get your girl. Now, I'll see you on the business side in a couple of weeks, but hopefully, my son will end this bullshit grudge and see me before then," Sebastian spoke his peace and hung up.

E-Love sat there feeling like shit. In his mind, he just knew that Leah had fucked his dad. It wasn't that he didn't trust Leah because she was a real one, but he knew that his dad was a straight up man. E-Love wanted to call Leah, but he felt like she might reject his ass. He clicked on Facebook app and went to her page. As he scrolled, he saw that Leah had been tagged in several posts this morning with people praying for her. He kept scrolling and saw that Leah had updated her picture of her parents and the caption said, *I love you both...until we meet again.*

"Damn man. My girl going through it and I'm acting stupid,"

E-Love knew that she had to be in Florida still, so he texted his travel agent and had her book him a flight and then he went and packed a bag. He felt like calling her, but that wouldn't do her any justice. E-Love needed to see her face to face. He needed to hold her.

Von Wiley Hall

Chapter Thirty-Seven

Rhap stared at herself in the mirror. It had been a couple of weeks since Swerve beat the fuck out of her, and she still had a few bruises on her caramel skin. She was in the bathroom staring at her reflection wondering what her life had become. That was the first time that Swerve had ever put his hands on her. On top of that, threatening her life put the icing on the cake. Living life in fear was never anything that Rhap imagined herself doing, but there she was.

Rhap thought about her cousin and felt bad. Leah called the day before and Rhap wanted to confide in her, but she couldn't say shit because Swerve was breathing down her neck. Rhap moved from mirror to mirror and turned on the shower. With each step she took, pain shot through her right side. The pains were worse when she took deep breaths, so she tried to avoid those at all cost. Swerve acted like he wanted to take her away to make up for all his mistakes and profess his love, but Rhap knew that he was just avoiding anyone that might try to visit, especially Leah. Rhap wanted to visit her aunt and uncle since they were in Florida, but she knew that she couldn't face them. She was ready to completely heal and get back to work, just to get away from Swerve. She was sure that he had been fired from his job, but he never kept one for long periods of time anyway and didn't give a fuck. Their money was separate, even though they had a joint account, and if she had to guess, he still had money from his mom's life insurance policy.

Rhap stepped into the shower and the hot water was painful, but she sucked it up and allowed the jets to message her skin. She had been taking lukewarm showers but was missing her hot water. Rhap figured the water might help her heal. Thoughts of Black entered her mind and she wondered if he has tried to contact her. The only time Swerve gave her the phone was when Leah called. Rhapsodee wished that she could go back to that day and she wouldn't have ever gone home. She stayed in the shower until the water began to turn cool.

Boom!
Boom!

Boom!

Rhap jumped at the sound of Swerve beating on the door. She knew that it wouldn't be long. Rhap rolled her eyes at his antics. She wondered what the fuck he thought she could be doing when he had her damn phone.

"What the fuck are you doing in there?" he based.

"Taking a shower. I'm getting out now," she said as sweetly as she could muster.

She knew that triggering him was only going to make him go into another one of his rages. He hadn't hit her since the incident two weeks ago, but he had pushed her and choked her, which had to be the reason she was still sore. She got out of the shower quickly as her body allowed her to and dried off. Rhap wrapped the towel around her body and exited the bathroom, bumping into Swerve. She hung her head low expecting the bullshit to start but instead, her phone rang from the nightstand. Rhap knew it was Leah by the ringtone, so she went and picked it up.

"Make it quick!" Swerve demanded.

"Hello," Rhap answered and she heard nothing but sniffles coming from Leah. "What's wrong Leah?' She queried, full of worry.

"Mom and dad. They're…gone," Leah sniffled.

"Gone? What you mean gone? Gone where Leah?" Rhap asked, knowing the answer but dreading it.

"Rhap, they died last night."

"Oh my God. Noooo! Not auntie and uncle! I'm so sorry, Leah. I'm on my way. I'm only like an hour away baby girl," Rhap panicked, trying to think of how she was going to hide her bruises because there was no way in hell she wasn't going to be with Leah.

"Where you think you goin'?" Swerve based after she hung up.

'Look, my aunt and uncles died. I have to go be there for my cousin. You aren't about to make me leave her all alone during this time," Rhap found courage from deep within and challenged Swerve. "Besides, don't you think people will know that something is really wrong if I'm not there for my family? I've only talked to my mom once and she probably doesn't even know yet. My God let me call her," Rhap started falling apart.

Swerve looked like he wanted to protest, but agreed that she could go, but he was going too. At that point, Rhap really didn't care, she just knew that she had to go and be by her cousin's side.

Two hours later, Rhap was on the passenger's side and Swerve was pulling into her aunt's driveway. Rhap lowered the sun visor on the rental car and opened the mirror so that she could make sure that the makeup was still covering her bruises. She had her phone during the drive, but she was only able to talk to her people because Swerve was listening, of course. Rhap hated to feel so weak, but she wasn't ready to die, so she continued doing what Swerve said. As soon as he parked, Rhap wasted no time getting out. Leah opened the door a few seconds after Rhap rang the doorbell. They fell into each other's arms and cried their hearts out. Rhap was hurting for her cousin, but she was also hurting herself. That was the first time that she had been able to let out a real cry and it was much needed.

"I got you Leah. I'm here for you!" Rhap comforted her.

They hugged each other a little while longer and they finally made their way to the couch.

"Mom has everything mapped out already, but I've been reading through their papers and making sure everything is still in order. I can't believe this. I was supposed to be coming to stay for a week at the end of the month. Dad waited until I got here before he died," Leah explained everything.

"It's sad, but you know with the type of love that they had, I'm not surprised that they died so close together," Rhap reasoned.

"Yeah, I actually thought about that too," Leah sighed.

"So, did auntie request for them to be taken back home? I gotta call mom back."

"Yeah she did. So, I'm looking at having their funerals Saturday. It's Tuesday, so we should be able to swing it."

"Yeah, we'll make it happen."

"So how much longer you here for work?" Leah asked and then Swerve walked in the door,

"Hey Leah. Sorry for your loss," he spoke.

"Thanks," Leah replied, but Rhap could tell she didn't want to."

"Can I use the bathroom?" Swerve asked and Leah pointed down the hall.

"I can leave whenever. I gotta be there for you. We're family," Rhap expressed.

"Swerve is here with you for work?" Leah queried with her eyebrows raised.

Rhap could feel Leah staring through her soul. When Leah reached up and lifted her chin up, Rhap knew that her cousin was about to go in. The only thing that saved her was the ringing of the doorbell.

Chapter Thirty-Eight

Swerve went to the bathroom so that he could answer his vibrating phone. He had stayed outside talking to Yoshi in an attempt to calm her down, but clearly the shit wasn't working. Swerve knew that she was going to spazz out. The first few days, she was fine because Swerve had her thinking that he was working overtime. That shit didn't last after day five though. Yoshi pretty much knew how long Rhap stayed at home and knew that she should have been at work. Swerve was about to talk to Yoshi while Rhap took her long as showers and when she was in the bedroom part of the suite, but it was mostly texting that they did.

"Are you on vacation with that bitch?" Yoshi fumed when he answered the phone.

"Huh? What are you talking about?"

"Cut the bullshit Swerve. I drove by your place and your car wasn't there. It hasn't been there all week. You haven't been at work either, so I drove to the airport, went through the parking lots and what did I find? Your fucking car!"

Swerve couldn't think of shit to say and he knew that his silence was about to prove Yoshi right. Even though it wasn't really a vacation, he knew that he had spoiled Yoshi by spending so much time with her, it didn't matter what the reason was, she wouldn't care.

"Yoshi, baby, calm down. You know you can't be stressing. I didn't want to tell you because I have to travel with Rhap because she had a family emergency. In fact, her aunt and uncle both died. You have to let me play my role until I can move on freely. I don't want any drama when I leave," Swerve explained.

"I'm getting sick of that excuse James St. John. Be at my house within twenty-four hours or you gon' see the other side!" Yoshi screamed and hung up.

Swerve stood there feeling like all of his shit was about to catch up with him. He had no intentions of leaving Rhap. He planned to continue living his double life in hopes that Yoshi would be happy with seeing him when Rhap was out of town working. There was an ounce of regret in his heart for beating Rhap, but only an ounce.

Swerve felt like that beating along with his threats would keep her in line. He had put too much fear within her in the past two weeks that it was time to get back to being the nice Swerve. Fucking with her mind is what he had been doing all along, so he felt like there was no need to stop now.

He pissed and then washed his hands. With the water still running, Swerve thought about what his next move should be. Keeping Yoshi in line had to be his main priority. So, Swerve stood there and decided that he would threaten Rhap one more time and then leave. It wasn't like he liked any of her family, anyway, so he wouldn't feel bad for leaving her.

He turned the water off and then exited the bathroom. Swerve made his way back to the hallway and heard the doorbell ringing. When he made it to the living room, Leah was opening the door and there stood E-Love. Swerve had been spotted by E-Love before doing dirt, and he instantly became paranoid.

"E-Love, what you…"

He heard Leah start talking, but E-love pulled her in for a hug.

Swerve took that as his opportunity to talk to his wife. She must have noticed the look of fake pity that he had displayed because she spoke up.

"What's wrong?" she made her way to him since Leah was occupied and was leading E-Love to the back.

"My boss just called. He needs me back tomorrow. We gotta leave babe," he whispered.

"I can't leave Leah. I won't leave her," Rhap folded her arms across her chest.

"Her lil boyfriend just made it," Swerve tried to lay it on thick.

"I'm her family!!"

"Okay, okay. Well I have to leave, but you need to remember every word that I've said. I'm sorry that things got to this point, but we're in this thing forever," he pulled her in for a hug.

Rhap tensed up and that was exactly what he needed from her. Fear.

"I'm gonna go on to the airport and catch a flight. Keep me posted on the details and let me know when y'all are on the way back," Swerve kissed her and left.

Swerve left in a hurry so that he could get back to Lithonia, playhouse and get his shit together.

*****

It was almost midnight when Swerve landed in Atlanta. There weren't any nonstop flights, so he had a layover in Jacksonville. He got off the plane and had his luggage within twenty minutes and headed outside. Before Swerve made it to the car, he could see that something was wrong. His suspicions were confirmed as he walked up on his car. Two of his tires had been flattened and the windshield and rear mirrors were broken. Swerve didn't want to turn into a woman beater, but he wanted to go and beat the fuck out of Yoshi because he knew she was the one who was responsible for fucking up his shit.

He pulled out his phone and called her. It rang and rang, he almost thought the voicemail was about to pick up, but Yoshi answered it in a groggy voice.

"Yoshi, why the fuck did you do this?" Swerve based.

She began sobbing and telling him how much she missed him and how emotional she was. Swerve could barely make out what she was saying, she was crying just that hard. If it wasn't for the fact that Yoshi was carrying his baby, Swerve would fuck her up.

"Come and get me from the airport!" he told her and hung up

Swerve told himself that she was about to suck the skin off his dick for the rest of the week to make up for her fuck up.

Von Wiley Hall

Chapter Thirty-Nine

Leah led E-Love to her room, that used to be her parents, to have a little privacy. She really didn't mind Rhap hearing anything, but it was Swerve who she didn't care to be in the presence of. Her emotions were all over the place. She was happy as hell to see E-Love, but also sad because of what had transpired between the two of them. As soon as they made it in the room, E-Love pulled her into his arms again and Leah completely melted.

"I got you babe. I got you! And I'm sorry. Please forgive me baby. I should have stayed and listened and not flew off the handle like that. I just couldn't shake the idea of my dad being with my woman. I love you so damn much and I never thought I'd be the jealous type, but I am. Especially over you. I'm sorry baby. Please forgive me. I promise I'll spend the rest of my life making this up to you," E-Love apologized for his actions while consoling her.

Leah wanted to reply to him, but she couldn't at that moment. She just wanted to enjoy his embrace because what she had to say might shift the entire atmosphere. E-Love held her for what seemed like an eternity and Leah finally lifted her head up.

"You forgive me?" E-Love asked

"E-Love, I'm very emotional right now and…"

'I know baby. I fucked up. I really fucked up. I should have listened."

"Yeah, but you didn't. So, what happens the next time something happens? You gonna shut me out and disappear? Out of all the shit I've put up from you and your lil bitches and we weren't even together, but you really wanted to call me a hoe without letting me explain," Leah expressed, letting her frustrations spill.

"Everything you're saying is right. I can't even front. Let me make it up to you. I miss you!" he pulled her back close to him.

Leah was conflicted as fuck. She didn't want to give in so fast, but she not only wanted E-Love, but she needed him. It appeared that her pussy needed him too and must have sensed his presence because she started getting moist as he held her. E-Love rubbed her back and then began palming her ass, causing soft moans to escape

Leah's lips. She was thankful that she had closed the door, but even if she hadn't Leah wouldn't have had one care in the world! Rhap had Swerve to occupy her for a few minutes. She couldn't fight it any longer. When E-Love started kissing her neck, she made her way to the bed. It would be the first time that she had sex in her parent's place, and she hoped that it wasn't true that the dead people could watch you because she needed her fix.

Leah was dressed in a tank top and a pair of lounge pants. She had really forgotten that she left clothes there. She blamed it on the fact that she knew something was wrong. E-Love pulled her tank top over her head and went straight for her erect nipples since she didn't have a bra on. He sucked and licked and devoured them as if he had really been missing them. Leah's juices were flowing, and her panties were drenched. E-Love slipped her pants down and rubbed her body. Leah tensed up a little because she was afraid that he might feel how hard her belly was. She knew that she needed to tell him, but she just needed to be fucked for the moment and would worry about telling him about her pregnancy later.

"Shiiiit!" Leah squealed when E-Love teased her clit with his tongue.

In no time at all, Leah was cumming. Her body had been missing the hell out of E-Love and it showed. Slow and easy, E-love filled her insides and Leah was in heaven. The connection she felt with him mixed with bomb as sex was enough to make any woman go crazy.

"You're so fuckin' wet baby!" E-Love grunted.

"You feel so good!" Leah moaned.

The way that he was making love to her made her fall deeper in love. Even though she kept telling herself not to forgive him so easy, the shit wasn't really working. E-Love hit her spot back to back, making her squirt.

"I was waiting on that shit!" E-Love flipped her over.

He beat her pussy up from the back. Leah threw it back on him and was keeping up until he reached around her and started massaging her pearl. She couldn't take it any longer, but he wasn't done with her. E-Love made up for lost time and emptied his seeds into

166

her ten minutes later. He collapsed down on the bed beside her and pulled her close to him.

"You got me all soft and shit, but I don't want to lose you. I promise I'll communicate better from here on out. I love you!" he told her.

"I love you too!" Leah replied

Just like that, all of the thoughts that she was having were gone. She laid there and was enjoying the moment until she thought about Rhap. Leah hopped up because she wanted to watch more of their interactions anyway.

"What's wrong?" E-Love asked.

"Something is going on with Rhap, and I gotta find out what it is. She had on makeup and she never wears makeup."

"So, you think sum' up because she got on makeup?" E-Love vacillated.

"Not just that, but she been gone for two weeks and she said she was at work, but why is he here? She wouldn't FaceTime me or nothing. And it looks like she is covering up marks. I know my cousin, something ain't and I need to see how they interact. She kinda tensed up when he walked in," Leah explained.

'Well I'ma let you handle that. I don't get in folk's relationships and shit," E-Love sat up.

"Well if he is putting his hands on my cousin, I'ma fuck him up," Leah fumed.

"Baby, you gon' force me to get into the shit if you do, so if possible, let your cousin handle it."

Leah heard what he was saying, and she knew what he meant, but she couldn't promise him anything because she had no idea how she might react. They both went into the bathroom and washed up. Leah was tempted to initiate round two because it was taking her mind off of everything, but she decided against it.

"I know that look, but I got you later baby. We need to go ahead and handle business. I'm here so I can be by your side," E-Love kissed her forehead.

"You're right. Mom left instructions and directions to every-where I gotta go. Let's get this over with," Leah sighed.

Leah made her way out and expected to see Rhapsodee and Swerve, but she only saw her cousin.

"Where's Swerve?"

"His job called, and he finally left," Rhap replied with a mixture of relief and agitation laced on her face.

"What's wrong Rhap?" Leah got straight to the point.

"Leah, you have enough on your plate, we'll talk later."

"No, what the punk ass nigga do?" Leah voices disapproval of Rhap's answer.

"Leah you know you shouldn't be getting worked up and shit," Rhap reasoned

She caught E-Love looking at her out of the corner of his eye.

"Girl I'm good, but don't try to change the subject."

"Ima leave the two of you alone and go grab my phone. Leah, we need to handle that business soon," E-Love interrupted them and then went out the front door.

"Spill it," Leah sat down beside her cousin.

"I'm scared Leah. I've never been so scared in my life," Rhap broke down and then her phone rang with Swerve's name popping up on the ID.

It was a FaceTime call and Rhap answered, so Leah knew that her cousin had been hiding a hell of a lot. She recoiled as she heard Swerve talking about his layover and how much he missed Rhap and shit. Leah cringed and she could tell by Rhap's fake ass replies that she wanted to do the same thing. After listening to them ramble for another minute or so Rhap finally hung up. She took a deep breath, made Leah promise not to tell anyone anything that she was about to say, and then ran everything down to her cousin. Leah listened to her cousin pour her heart out without interrupting her. She wanted to kill Swerve with her bare hands. Leah knew Swerve was a notch ass nigga, but she never in a million years expected him to put his hands on Rhap and threaten her life. She couldn't blame her cousin for being scared because Swerve had shown her a different side of him and everything was possible.

168

Leah had tears of her own while Rhap talked. Leah hated that she made her cousin that promise because she really wasn't sure if she was going to be able to hold up to her end of the bargain.

"Listen to me. Let's get through this week, and then we're gonna get you outta this shit. I promise you. As much as I hate to say it, just play by the rules for now, and we will be thinking of a plan. I already have something in mind. You're not in this alone, Rhap, okay? I love you," Leah comforted her cousin and started putting a plan together in her head to help get her out of the bullshit.

Von Wiley Hall

Chapter Forty

Having a solid team was detrimental, especially in the line of work that E-Love was involved in. He couldn't be more grateful for having a partner like Black and right-hand man like Bobby B. E-Love had been by Leah's side since he saw that posts on her page. They were currently back Atlanta and Leah was sound asleep in his bed. The wake was a couple of hours ago and the funeral was the next day. Even though Leah's parents had moved away, it was evident that there were still loved and respected just by the turnout at the wake. E-Love had never been by a woman's side during a time of need like he was with Leah, but he was glad to be her rock.

E-Love grabbed his phone and keys and then headed out. Their flight arrived back late the night before and they went shopping that morning. Everything was situated and it was time for E-Love to handle a little business. As soon as he hopped in the car, his phone rang.

"Hey Ma!"

"Eric, have you made up with that sweet Leah yet? I want to bring her down for dinner next weekend so we can have a do over."

"Yeah, we good ma, but I don't think that's a good idea. Leah just lost both of her parents and the funeral is tomorrow. I'm not sure how she'll be feeling."

"Oh, my goodness. What's the address to the church? I can send some flowers. That's sad."

E-Love told his mom that he would text her the details. They talked for a few more minutes and then he hung up, sending the information as promised. Since his mom was so talkative, E-Love pulled up to his destination a few minutes after hanging up with her. When E-Love pulled on the block, he didn't see shit but blue lights. Instead of parking, he kept driving by so that he could see what was going on. When E-Love saw Bobby B being led out in handcuffs, he almost stopped, but he knew the rules. If anyone was ever arrested, they all knew that it wasn't wise to show their faces at the same time.

"What the fuck happened?" he fumed to himself.

He kept driving and prayed that the spot was clean like it should have been. He trusted his boy to keep shit on task, but that didn't mean someone else couldn't have fucked up. E-Love picked his phone up and made a call to Travis, the cop on their payroll. After telling him what he has just witnessed, E-Love hung up and the only thing that he could do was impatiently wait on more details. Since it was Friday night, there was a strong possibility that Bobby B would have to sit over the weekend, but he hoped that wasn't the case.

Not wanting to get caught up in any bullshit, E-Love send a text to the team from his burner and told them to shut everything down. Once that was done, he headed back to play the waiting game. When he pulled into his driveway, his phone rang.

"Give me some good news, man!"

"I wish I could. This looks like some bullshit ass game the city cops are playing. They ain't even processed him yet and they don't take long to process niggas. Your boy might have to sit a few hours, but I got my people on it," Travis explained.

"I'ma be tied up all day tomorrow, so try to get this shit handled tonight. I ain't paying you for nothing," E-Love based and hung up.

He was frustrated as fuck. Just when he thought everything was going smooth, some bullshit happened. E-Love made his way inside and poured a double shot of Henny. After he gulped it down, he stripped out of his clothes and climbed in the bed with Leah. He tried not to wake her, but she woke up anyway and scooted close to him.

"E-Love?"

"Yeah baby?"

"After all of this is over, I gotta tell you something okay?"

"Good or bad?"

"Just depends on how you view it. I wanna get through tomorrow first though," Leah sadly expressed.

"Aight baby. Get some rest," he kissed her on the forehead and tried to get some rest of his own but knowing that it would be impossible.

Hard and Ruthless

E-Love had his arm wrapped around Leah as she said her final goodbye to her parents. The service had ended, and they were at the cemetery awaiting that dreadful moment where the caskets would be lowered into the ground. E-Love thought back to his homie's funeral where he had to do shit after he was the one to pull the trigger. Funerals in Florida didn't happen like the ones he had witnessed in Georgia. It was like a party, but Leah reassured him that most repasts turned into parties. They both placed roses on each casket, and then Rhap followed suit along with some other people E-Love had met the day before.

They turned to leave and E-Love damn near bumped into his mom and sister.

"What y'all doing here?" he was surprised to see them there.

"We wanted to be here for Leah," his sister said and then her and his mom took turns giving her hugs.

The smile that was in Leah's face was one of genuine happiness. He could tell that she was surprised and elated to see his family, it made E-Love think about his dad wanting the three of them to sit down and talk. E-Love wasn't sure that was a good idea, but he knew that eventually they all needed to talk.

"It's so good to see y'all. I thought y'all was gonna hate me," Leah fretted.

"Girl no. We love you," Meek beamed, and his mom agreed.

"Is this a pregnant glow?" his mom asked Leah.

E-Love looked at Leah and the look on her face told him all that he needed to know.

"E-Love, remember I said that I needed to tell you something after the funeral. Well, this is what I wanted to tell you. Yes, I'm pregnant," Leah confirmed his mom's suspicion and turned to E-Love, searching for his reaction.

"Oh my God! I'm going to be a grandma finally! Thank you, Sweetheart."

Listening to his mom and sister's joyous reactions to the baby news, E-Love pulled Leah into him, hugging her tightly. "Damn, I can't say a nigga ever thought about having kids, but just like everything else, you have my black ass doing things I never expected to do. I'm about to be somebody's daddy. No worries baby, I got you and the baby!" he finally gave a reply. Leah was finally able to relax about being pregnant because she was slick worried about how E-Love was going to react to the news. She was glad that he accepted the news instead of flying off the handle with straight bullshit.

Hard and Ruthless

Chapter Forty-One

It had been two months since everything went left and Rhap was still going through the motions. The good thing about it, she didn't have long notice before she would be free. With the help of Leah, Rhap had found an apartment in Birmingham. Within the next couple of weeks, furniture would be delivered, and the electricity would be turned on. Rhap felt like she deserved an Oscar for the acting skills that she had been displaying lately. She literally couldn't stand the ground that Swerve walked on anymore, but she knew that she had to have patience in order for the plan to be executed properly.

Rhap had only taken on three work assignments since the incident, and Swerve had been with her on each of them. He swore his boss loved him and let him have his way, but Rhap wouldn't be surprised if his ass wasn't even working. She couldn't wait until she could get back to her life. Even when she moved, she knew that she was going to be looking over her shoulders, but with time, it would get better. Leah wanted her to go further away, but she figured that she needed to be near home in case anything happened. Moving one state over was not too close, but not too far.

Since Swerve was at work and Rhap hadn't seen her parents since the funeral, she convinced her mom to meet her at the Bone Fish & Grill, so that they could feed their faces. That restaurant had some of the best food ever and it had been a while since Rhap had eaten there. Her dad was working, so he would have to miss out. Her parents weren't together anymore, but they had grown and matured enough to be in the same settings on various occasions. Rhap didn't mind because the last time she saw him, he grilled her, asking what was wrong. Rhap was thankful that they weren't alone, and she was able to avoid him because he has a way of seeing right through her. Just to keep shit going smooth, Rhap texted Swerve back to let him know what she was doing. He didn't reply back before she got out of the car and Rhap didn't care one way or the other.

"Hey mom!" Rhap opened her mom's car door and then bent down and hugged her.

"Hey baby. You happy to see me, huh? I couldn't even get out the car first," her mom laughed.

"Of course, I am. I wish dad could've made it, but that old man gonna work forever."

"Chile, your daddy is the type who will die if he quits working, so let him work on," they shared a laugh, knowing what a workaholic he was.

They made their way inside and within ten minutes, they were halfway done with their first plates. The food was so good, and they weren't even talking about anything besides what they wanted on their next plate. Rhap knew that she was going to have to tell her parents that she was moving, but she just didn't want to disclose the real reason.

"What's wrong, Rhapsodee?" Brenda asked, concern lacing her voice vividly.

"What do you mean what's wrong?"

"Even though this food is really good, that's not what's really on your mind. I know you think your dad is the only one who really knows you, but remember, I carried you for nine months and went through fifteen hours of labor to get you here."

"Well dang, mom. Just read me then," Rhap laughed.

"Read you?"

"Don't worry about it, but I do have something to tell you."

"I knew something was in your mind. What's going on?"

"I'm moving to Birmingham,"

"Moving? You're a traveling nurse. What sense does it make for you to move? Unless you found a job there. And did you mean we instead of I'm?" Brenda continued.

"I said it right. I don't think Swerve wants to move, but I'm ready for a fresh start."

"Rhapsodee Daniels, I'm not even going to ask any question because it'll only make you lie more. With everything that's going on, especially with your favorite cousin being pregnant, I'm not buying that, but just know that when you're ready to be honest, I'm sure for you sweetheart,"

Rhap wanted so badly to tell her mom what was going on, but she couldn't take the chance of messing up her plans. She knew that her mom wouldn't tell her dad right away, and she didn't want her dad in jail for killing Swerve. She didn't want anyone caught up in her bullshit, but she had to tell at least one person to keep from going crazy, and she had already confided in Leah. Rhap changed the subject and started talking about vacations. Her parents hadn't been anywhere in a couple of years, so she was going to plan separate vacations for them unless they wanted to go together. Even though her parents weren't together anymore, they still kept a close friendship. They finished up with their meal and then decided to go and do a little shopping.

Rhap ended up buying more stuff for Leah's baby than she did for herself. She would be finding out what she was having at her next appointment and Rhap was positive that it was a girl. When she left her mom, she made one last stop by KFC to get Swerve something to eat since it was almost seven o'clock. Tine had really gotten away from her, but she enjoyed her mother-daughter day. After paying for and retrieving the chicken, Rhap left and headed home. When she passed by Arby's, thoughts of Black invaded her mind. She knew that he was too done with her and she couldn't blame him. Rhap wished that she still had his number, but apparently, Swerve had deleted it from her phone. The day they spent together was one of the best days of her life and she would cherish it forever.

After sitting in the car for a few minutes, Rhap decided that it was to get out and head inside. She put all of her bags in her arms and then made her way to the door. It was silent, which meant that Swerve must have parked in the back and just went inside. Making her way inside, Rhap heard him on the phone.

"Don't start that shit today. You gotta give me time! The more I do, the more you …"

He turned around and locked eyes with Rhap and then ended the phone call that he was on. She was already over his ass, but he had another thing coming if he thought she was stupid. Rhap dropped her bags and then stepped towards Swerve ready to cuss him the fuck out, but he beat her to the punch.

"Where the fuck you been?" he based.

"Who the fuck you talking to?" she retorted

"Who the fuck you think you talking to? You don't ask me no gotdam questions!" he stepped towards her.

"I'm talking to you! I'm sicka yo shit. Clearly you talking to a bitch and I'm over this. We can cut our losses right now and..."

Before Rhap could finish her sentence, Swerve's hands were wrapped around her throat.

"So, you want me to kill you, huh?" he gritted and squeezed tighter.

Rhap felt herself getting ready to pass out. She reached deep within her soul and found the strength to kick Swerve in his balls. He yelped out in pain and bent over. That gave Rhap just enough time to grab the vase that was on the coffee table and hit Swerve upside his big ass head. When he fell to the floor, she grabbed her phone and keys and ran for her life. The plan had to be improvised, but Rhap was fed the fuck up over James St. John. Her mom calling her by her maiden name during their lunch was the confidence that she needed to get back to being her true self.

Chapter Forty-Two

Even though he was in pain, Swerve got up, grabbed his keys, and did a light jog out the door. Rhap had grown some balls and he didn't like the shit one bit. Putting his hands on her again was something that he didn't plan on doing, but she triggered him, and he couldn't resist the shit. In his mind, all she had to do was be a good wife by doing what the fuck he said. Swerve drove like a bat outta hell out of the complex. Once he was out, he made a couple of turns and then he saw her car ahead stuck at a red light.

"Bingo!" he grinned and pressed on the gas harder.

The light turned to green before he got there and Rhap took off. She must have seen him speeding toward her because she sped up. Swerve was closing the gap, but another traffic was right ahead. Rhap flew through it turned yellow, and Swerve pressed the gas harder but not before the light changed.

Wham!!

Swerve's car was knocked into another car and he flipped a couple of times before everything faded to black.

*****

When Swerve opened his eyes, the brightness forced him to shut them back instantly. He finally adjusted to the light and sat up. His head was banging, and he didn't know why. It was then that Swerve noticed he was in the hospital. A beeping noise sounded from the IV and a few moments later, a nurse walked in.

"Oh, you're awake. Let me get the doctor," the nurse cheerfully stated and turned to leave.

Swerve tried to stop her, but she must not have heard him. Everything began to flood his mind at once and he remembered the accident he had while chasing Rhap.

"Fuck. I gotta get outta here," he got up but ended up bending over in pain.

"Oh Mr. St, John, you shouldn't be up. Get back in bed. You have quite a few injuries," the nurse helped him back in bed.

"Mr. St. John, you gave us quite a scare. You've been out a whole week.

"A week?" Swerve interrupted.

Tthe doctor went on to explain the injuries Swerve had incurred, but he wasn't listening. The only thing that was on his mind was finding his wife. The last thing the doctor said was that he would have to stay for a couple of more days but that wasn't about to happen. The doctor dismissed himself and the nurse stayed and gave Swerve another dose of meds.

'Where are my belongings?" he asked her.

"They're actually right over there on the counter. As bad as you're banged up, I'm surprised your phone didn't break, but it's probably dead. I have an iPhone charger you can use.

"Fuck that phone. I'm just happy to be alive, but I think I need a nap.

"Yes, you should get as much rest as possible. Hit that button if you need me," the nurse smiled and left.

Swerve waited for a few minutes and then he limped over to where his belongings were, took the hospital gown off, and put his clothes on. There was some blood on his shirt, but he didn't care. Leaving the hospital in a gown was going to be damn dear impossible, so he had to put his clothes on. He picked up the phone and surprisingly the battery wasn't dead. It was on eight percent and he just knew that just about all two hundred and fifteen messages were more than likely from Yoshi and he was right. Swerve didn't have time to focus on that. He had to get gone. He requested an Uber and was notified that a driver was only three minutes away. Swerve made his way out of the door and thankfully, he didn't see the nurse. It wasn't until he got all the way in the hall that he noticed he was at Grady Hospital. Swerve knew he could leave against medical advice, but he just didn't want to go through the trouble of signing any papers or answering any question. He made it downstairs when his phone rang. It was the Uber driver calling and Swerve saw the Black Honda Civic pulling up. He hopped inside and got settled. If luck were on his side, Rhap would be at home waiting on him.

Swerve didn't even know he had fallen asleep until the car stopped. It had to be the pain meds. The only thing that he hated about leaving the hospital was that he didn't get a prescription, but he knew that he could get it later. He had shit to do that couldn't wait. Swerve got out of the car without saying thanks and made his way to his condo. The door was wide open when Swerve made it, and he heard movement as soon as he stepped inside.

"Who the fuck up in my shit?" he based as he walked through the doors.

"This definitely finna only be yo shit in just a few," Leah appeared from the back with an arm full of clothes.

She placed them in a box and that's when Swerve noticed that all of Rhap's belongings were being boxed up.

"What the hell are you doing? You not taking shit outta here!" Swerve ran up on Leah.

"You touch her, and I'll beat yo muthafuckin' ass!" E-Love appeared and calmly stated.

Swerve didn't do shit but fall back while Leah, E-Love and another guy he didn't know walked out with Rhap's things. He wanted to as where she was, but he knew better than to ask such a stupid question. Swerve wasn't about to let Rhap just leave him like that. He had worked too damn hard to keep his double life running and he planned on continuing that shit forever.

*****

Yoshi was in Target, picking through baby items that were on the clearance rack. She still didn't know what she was having, but the stuff was so cheap that it didn't even matter if she wouldn't be able to use it. Her next doctor's appointment was in a couple of weeks and she couldn't wait to see if she was having a girl. Yoshi heard someone sniffling and saw a lady appeared to be crying.

"Are you okay?" Yoshi inquired.

"Not really, but I don't wanna bother you with my problems," the lady sighed.

"I'm actually a good listener," Yoshi smiled.

For some reason, she felt like the lady needed a friend. Since all of her friends were a couple hours away, she wanted to befriend someone close by. There were times when she was lonely because of the lifestyle she had chosen to live, but she knew that it would be different after the baby was born. Even though she considered Swerve to be her best friend, it would do her good to have a female friend near.

"My boyfriend beat me and caused me to have a miscarriage. I was just about to enter my second trimester. It's all so fresh. I shouldn't have stopped by this section, but I just couldn't help myself," the lady sobbed.

"Oh my God! I'm so sorry!!" Yoshi felt sorry for her. The lady started crying even harder and Yoshi walked up to her and gave her a hug. Yoshi thought long and hard about what she wanted to say next. Before she changed her mind, she went ahead and said it.

"I'm new to the area and I don't know a lot of people. You wanna come over and hang out? We don't have to talk about babies," Yoshi suggested.

"I would love that. I'm new to the area as well and got tangled up with the wrong man."

"Great. Let me get your name and number and I'll text you."

"My number is 770-327-8104 and my name is Sharon."

Chapter Forty-Three

It was the fourth of July, which fell on a damn Wednesday, but Leah was in the passenger's seat while E-Love was driving and headed to his mom's. It was going to be a turnaround trip, but Leah was looking forward to some good food. She briefly thought about their trip, which was a few months ago.

"I'm so ready to eat some of your mom's good cookin'. Hopefully today is smooth,' Leah said after she finished texting Rhap.

She missed her cousin terribly, but she was happy that she was away from that trifling as husband of her.

"Yeah it's gon' be a smooth day, and I'm ready to grub myself. Got some business to handle first though," E-Love replied.

Leah decided to ignore his comment about business. She was ready to feed her face.

"I really miss Rhap, but I'm glad she is safe now. I knew Swerve's ass was a hoe, but I didn't know he was a woman beater. If you ev…"

"Aye, don't compare me to that punk ass nigga. He beat her ass though?" E-Love caught on to what she admitted.

"Yeah. I thought it was something like a shove and a slap or something, but when I went over to help shop for décor, she broke down and showed me the pictures she snuck and took and emailed herself. I'm glad she took them so she can use them for the divorce."

"Damn. That's fucked up. But for the record, you ain't gotta worry 'bout no shit like that," E-Love assured her.

Leah rubbed her protruding belly. She was five months and was really showing. It seemed like she had gotten huge overnight and she didn't understand why. The baby had a strong ass heartbeat at her last appointment, but he or she was stubborn as hell and they couldn't tell her the sex of the baby. She has an appointment the next day and was hoping to find out so she could start shopping. Her friends wanted to throw her a gender reveal party, but Leah told them just wait and do a baby shower. She knew that they would buy gifts, and she was trying to keep them from doing too much. Her phone chimed and when the messages started coming back to back,

Leah knew it was the group chat. She chatted with Twin, Princess and Rhap's crazy asses until E-Love pulled up to his mom's house.

"Ready baby?" he asked.

"Yup. We're starving," she wasted no time getting out.

"Greedy ass." E-Love laughed, and Leah playfully punched him once she was close to him.

He led the way inside and Leah followed him. Music could be heard coming from the backyard, so Leah was confused as to why E-Love was going inside. Once they made it in the house, no one was in the living room and he pulled her to the bathroom.

'Come on. We ain't got long before somebody comes knocking. I woulda went in my old room, be we got family staying here for the holiday and shit," E-Love pulled her dress up and began fumbling with her panties.

"Wait, boy, you tryna get a quickie in while all these people here?"

By the time Leah was done asking him that, he had her panties down at her ankles and when he lifted her leg, they came off. E-Love was inside of her and she was moaning before she could even fake protest.

"Umm, shit boy," Leah dug her nails into his back at that only seemed to make him go harder.

"This shit so good," E-Love grunted and fucked Leah harder.

She felt her juices running down her legs and she just knew that she was about to fall, but E-Love held her up.

Knock!

Knock!

Knock!

"Shhh." E-Love put his hand over her mouth.

"E-Love? Is that you? Oooh y'all nasty. I'm telling ma!" Meek laughed.

"Meek shut the hell up! We'll be out in a minute."

Leah tried to push him back, but E-Love held her still and started back stroking her. A couple of minutes later, he was done, and they were both washing off.

"Yo nasty as just had to get some."

"You wanted it too, girl."

Leah ignored him and fixed her messy bun that she had on top of her head. Her braids were out, and she planned on getting them done right away. She had to miss her appointment to help Rhap and her cousin was booked up. She would definitely be getting them done soon as someone canceled. Leah didn't care what day it was, she was going to make it happen. They made their way outside and Meek was in the kitchen getting something out of the refrigerator. Leah stopped in her tracks because she was embarrassed as hell.

"Girl, Meek ain't no damn body. Come on," E-Love pulled her forward.

"Heeyy Leah girl. I ain't gone pick at y'all high school acting asses too much," she laughed and hugged Leah.

"Blame your brother," Leah chuckled.

"Oh, I do, but since you here, come on and let's kick some ass on these spades," Meek pulled her away from E-Love.

Leah and Meek had run a wheel on one team and were up on the next game when they heard, "It's time to eat".

"Okay everybody. We 'bout to eat, but my soon to be daughter-in-law gets the first plate, so the rest of y'all hungry asses just fall back. Come on baby," she motioned for Leah to move to the front of the line.

She got up and looked around for E-Love, when she spotted him, he was talking to his dad. That was the first time that Leah had laid eyes on his dad since the Easter cookout. She had been to the house a few times for dinner, but he had never been in attendance. Surprisingly, it wasn't as awkward as she thought it would be, and since E-Love seemed to be in a good mood, she didn't have any worries, Leah piled her plate with food and grabbed a bottle of water, and then went and sat back down. The first thing she took a bite of was the mac-n-cheese and a piece of rib.

"Open your eyes while you eat girl," E-Love suddenly appeared, laughing.

Leah couldn't do shit but laugh. Her eyes had to be closed because she didn't even see him walk up.

The rest of the day went smooth. E-Love even initiated a conversation between his dad and Leah, breaking the ice after they finished eating. The whole day was great, and they hit the road heading back home around eight that night, anticipating the next day.

*****

Princess: *call us on group FaceTime when they get ready to do the sonogram.*
Twin: *Yeah do that please. I'm tryna know when y'all know.*
Rhap: *I really wish I could be there.*
Leah: *Y'all want me in the doctor's office being ghetto huh? And I know Rhap, but the shower is in a couple of months and hopefully shit will be smoother, and you can come.*
Rhap: *I'm coming regardless, Fuck Swerve!*
Princess: *I never thought I'd see the day when you said those words Rhap.*
Rhap: *me either, but with everything that happened, it can't be repaired. Have you heard anything from that bitch Sharon?*
Twin: *I gotta go back on her page and see what she been up to.*
Leah: *We're pulling up y'all. I'll get back up with y'all in a few.*

After thirty minutes later, Leah vitals had been taken and she had answered all of the routine questions and had her cervix checked. Everything was fine. She had gained a hell of a lot of weight and mentally told herself that she had to cut back. According to baby books, the average weight for a woman to gain during pregnancy was twenty pounds and she was already up to eighteen and had four months to go. As she laid back waiting on the ultrasound tech, Leah thought about how she was going to smash her plate of leftovers, once they got back home, forgetting about how was had just told herself she was cutting back.

"Ms. Fuquay, are we ready to see if the little one is going to participate today?" the tech walked in and asked.

"Yep, we're ready," Leah beamed.

"If it doesn't work this time, we can do a blood test to determine the sex."

"Hmmm, I guess we can decide that later," Leah looked at E-Love and he told her that he was good with whatever she wanted.

The tech rubbed the cold gel on her stomach and Leah wiggled a little.

"Oh my God!" the tech said, scaring the shit out of Leah and E-Love.

Von Wiley Hall

Chapter Forty-Four

"What's wrong? E-Love stood up and Leah sat up.

'I'm sorry for scaring you guys. The volume was down on this machine, and I didn't hear a heartbeat, but I hope you guys are prepared for the news..."

"What news?" Leah asked in a quiet voice.

"Look right here," the tech pointed.

"What are we looking at?" E-Love wondered as he looked at the area the tech referenced to.

"It looks like we had a little baby, hiding behind the other one. You guys are having twins," the tech exclaimed.

"Twins!?!?" E-Love and Leah screamed in unison.

"Yes, fraternal twins, the little girl is behind her brother and she couldn't hide any longer. Congratulations!!" she beamed.

The only thing that could be heard in the room was the babies' heartbeats. E-Love was in total shock. Having twins had never crossed his mind at all, and apparently Leah's either, but the more he stood there and thought, a smile invaded his face.

"What we gon' do with twins??" Leah shrieked.

"Baby, we'll be fine. Think about it, you just lost your mom and dad, now look, we got a boy and a girl. They can't replace them, but they're gonna bring some joy to our family," E-Love expressed.

He could tell that his words were sinking in. A single tear rolled down Leah's left cheek. He leaned over and kissed it away and then planted a kiss on her lips.

"Thank you, baby," she told him, and they hugged.

The sonogram tech printed off pictures for them and the twins were labeled Baby A and Baby B. E-Love helped Leah up after the tech wiped her stomach off and they prepared to leave. After Leah scheduled her appointment for the next month, they left the clinic and made their way to the car. E-Love could have sworn he saw that nigga Swerve walking towards the back with some female, but he didn't alert Leah because he wasn't with the drama. Just the thought of Swerve reminded E-Love of some shit he needed to do.

"What you want to eat?" he asked Leah after he cranked up.

"You know we got some leftovers," she reminded him.

"So, you telling me them leftovers gon' last for the rest of the day? It ain't even twelve yet."

"Okay you're right. I'll eat that tonight. Let's grab some Mickey D's," Leah suggested it because he hadn't had a Big Mac in a while. E-Love felt his phone vibrating, so he pulled it from his pocket. He saw that it was an unknown number with a 912-area code, but he didn't answer because he didn't know who it was. The number had actually called a couple days before, but they didn't leave a message. As soon as the phone stopped ringing, it started ringing again. E-Love went ahead and answered because he didn't want Leah to think that he was ignoring calls and shot because she was with him.

"Hello."

"Oh, so you finally decided to answer the phone?" Mya snapped in his ear.

"Who is this?" E-Love asked, knowing good and well who it was.

"You wanna play games huh?"

"Sorry you got the wrong number," E-Love hung up and discreetly blocked the number.

Thankfully, Leah was texting and wasn't paying him any attention. E-Love figured that she was in her group chat breaking the news to her girls because she kept laughing out loud every other second. He knew that he needed to get a handle on Mya soon and very soon though. E-Love had no idea what she could have wanted anyway. They didn't even fuck. He pulled up to the restaurant a little while later and then went inside and retrieved their orders. Neither one of them waited until they made it home before digging into their food. E-Love knew that he had some shit to handle, so he wasn't going to be able to sit down and eat anyway.

"You know you gotta take it extra easy now right?"

"E-Love, I'm already taking it easy. Don't start," he could tell Leah was rolling her eyes by how she said it.

"Like I said, you gon' have to take it extra easy, so you can kill the lil attitude. Good thing you pretty much your own boss."

"I hear ya baby," she replied in a nicer tone.

*****

Later that evening, E-Love and Black had just finished up a meeting and they were shooting the shit. Black had taken care of the problem in Birmingham and E-Love was a tad bit disappointed that he didn't get to put the work in on the muthafucka that had shot at them, but nonetheless, he was happy that the situation was resolved.

"Man listen, let me tell you 'bout this shit. I ain't supposed to mention it, but I think you need to call your girl," E-Love advised.

"Who?"

"Nigga you know who! Rhap. Your future wife according to you. Man, she been going through it. We helped her move and everything, but nobody knows except her lil small circle."

"Going through it, how?" black questioned.

"Bruh, that nigga beat her and shit. That probably was his bitch ass that texted you that shit that had you in your feelings. I knew that didn't sound like the Rhap I knew. But forget that for now, I just feel like you need to hit her up. She in your area too. Well, she works outta town, but we set her up in Birmingham," E-Love explained.

"When all this happen?"

"Shit started a couple of months ago."

"And you just now telling me?" Black fumed.

"I told you to hit her up before nigga."

"Yeah, but I thought it was on some matchmaker type shit. You ain't said shit 'bout all this!"

"Just call ya girl man."

"I deleted her damn number," Black admitted.

"I'll get it from Leah. She wants you and Rhap together so bad anyway."

E-Love could tell that the news he has just delivered to his friend made him feel some type of way. He had been meaning to tell him. But his shit was fucked up around that time too and then the death of Leah's parents was a lot. He just hoped his boy made it right because he knew Rhap was a good girl. They had a few more drinks and then parted ways. E-Love was tempted to call Mya and find out what it was that she wanted but decided that he would deal with that another day.

The news that E-Love delivered had Black's head fucked up. He felt like shit for shutting his queen out at a fucked-up time that she needed him the most. It was a little after seven when Black made it back to Birmingham. Sosa called him before he made it home. He had made up his mind that he couldn't wait for E-Love. He was about to log on his AT&T account and find Rhap's phone number in his history.

"What up?" he answered.

"I need you to drop me off at the airport right quick man." Sosa requested.

"Man, you can't catch an Uber. I got some shit to figure out."

"Niggaa. Come drop me off right quick. The Uber said fifteen minutes and I gotta catch this flight."

"Aight man damn. I'll be there in a minute," Black ended the call.

Thirty minutes later, Black was turning into the airport. His mind was so distracted that he turned into the arriving flight terminal and Sosa told him to stop because he didn't have time for him to circle back around. A shuttle was passing by and Sosa ran out in front of it and hopped on. Black laughed at his ass and kept it moving. When he passed by the Delta tunnel, he hit the brakes so fast. He just knew that his eyes were playing tricks on him. He pulled over and parked, turned his blinkers on, and hopped out. She was tapping away into her phone, but when he got close it was like she felt his presence because Rhap looked up at him, just staring. Black was nervous as hell because he couldn't read the expression that was on her face.

Chapter Forty-Five

She felt his presence and smelled his cologne before she saw him. Rhapsodee looked up and locked eyes with Black and her heart skipped a beat. She didn't know if she was dreaming or if he was really standing there staring back at her. Rhap had just landed from a three-week work assignment and she was in the process of requesting an Uber. It was crazy as hell that she had just has a dream about him while on the plane, and there he was. Her eyes began to water as Black made his way over to her and pulled her in for a hug.

"I missed you so much baby, and I'm sorry I didn't try harder to contact you."

Rhap couldn't stop the tears that fell from her eyes. She missed Black so much and thought that he hated her. Swerve had turned her life upside down, and she never thought that she could ever entertain another man, but there she was, damn near in love with one who seemed like a breath of fresh air.

"It's not your fault. It's really all my fault and I'm sorry. I thought you hated me once I didn't hear from you anymore," Rhap admitted.

"I could never hate you Rhapsodee. In fact, this time apart has only made me realize that I love you. I don't know how that shit happened so fast, but I'm gonna spend the rest of my life making you happy," he held her chin and made her look him in the eyes.

"It's crazy because I feel like I love you too," Rhap confessed. "But I have so much to tell you," she continued.

"Let's get out of here before they tow my car and we can talk," Black ushered her to his car.

After he opened the door for her and helped her in, he put her luggage in the back and then hopped behind the wheel, leaving right as one of the security guards was walking up.

"You hungry?" he asked.

"Actually I am. I kinda got a taste for seafood," she mentioned.

"A woman who knows what she wants to eat. I can get used to this," Black laughed.

They ended up at Pappadeaux's and Rhapsodee had no idea what Black did, but they bypassed the long line and were seated and served right away. It was like they hadn't skipped a beat. Rhap was so carefree with him that she found herself pouring her heart out about everything in her life. She even confessed things that she tried to forget from the beginning of their marriage, leaving no stones unturned even about her flaws. Black listened without interrupting her, and when she was done, he spoke, and it was her turn to listen.

"Everything that you've gone through had to happen in order for you to get to this point. Every ounce of heartache and pain, and even the good times that you thought you had. You blame yourself for the actions of a grown ass man and that shit gotta stop. I'm pissed off at how the fuck boy treated you, but I'm gonna show you how a real man treats his woman. You don't have to look over your shoulders anymore, I got you. To ensure you're safe, you're staying with me, and I'm not taking no for an answer."

Rhap didn't even know how to respond to him. There really wasn't even anything to say or do but agree and that was exactly what she did. The way that Black spoke, he was loving, yet firm and Rhap already felt protected. They ate as much as they could and then Rhap got a to-go box to take the rest of her food to go.

"I have several different places, but this is where I rest my head when I want peace, and you're the only woman who has ever been here," Black told her as he made his way down a long driveway.

It was dark outside, but Rhap could still see how immaculate the estate was. If the outside were that beautiful, she couldn't wait to see how the inside was.

"Your mom hasn't been here?" Rhap quizzed after he parked.

"Nope, you're the only woman. I haven't even fully furnished the place and my mom lives in New Jersey," Black explained.

They got out of the car and made their way to the front door. Black unlocked the door and stepped to the side so she could go in. Rhap took it upon herself to flip the light switch on and she was in awe at the sight before her. Black was right that the house wasn't fully furnished, but she felt like she was standing in a magazine or something.

194

Hard and Ruthless

"Your home is beautiful!" she complimented.

"This gon' be ours, unless you want something different," he wrapped his arms around her.

"Boy, you say all the right stuff, but you know I got a lot of shit to handle," Rhap expressed when she thought about her situation.

"All you gotta do is get paperwork in motion and let me do the rest."

Black gave Rhap a tour of the house and told her that she could have her way decorating. They stayed up until almost five o'clock the next morning talking and having fun.

It felt like they had known each other all of their lives. The way that she felt was indescribable. Rhap couldn't lie, in the back of her mind, it seemed like shit was too good to be true. She felt like Black was genuine, but thoughts of Swerve rearing his ugly head plagued her mind and Black finally asked her what was wrong. She expressed her true feelings without holding back and Black assured her that he had her back. He made a promise to protect her at all costs. She closed her eyes and hung unto his every word. As the sun was rising, Rhap fell asleep in Black's arms with a sense of peace.

Von Wiley Hall

Chapter Forty-Six

Swerve almost shit a brink when he walked into Yoshi's house a month ago and saw Sharon sitting at the kitchen table. She played it smooth while Yoshi was in the room and then started her shit when Yoshi went to the bathroom, the same shit she did with Rhap. Swerve didn't know what the fuck her problem was until she texted him the words that he said to her after he fucked her at the strip club. For the past few weeks, when he wasn't searching for Rhap, Swerve had been plotting on how he could get rid of Sharon. For good. Once he has her out of the way, he could go harder looking for his wife.

A text came through on Swerve's phone, but he ignored it. He had to remain focused. It was a hot ass August night, and he was anxious to get his plan in motion. Right on cue, Sharon walked out of Dudley's twenty minutes after three. Sharon didn't lock her car doors, making it easy for him to enter. He had been watching and waiting for her stalking as. Swerve was free because Yoshi and J.J. were visiting her mom for the weekend. Her mom hated Swerve just like Big Posse, so Swerve kept his distance. Quiet as kept, he was happy about it because it was during times like the present that he had time to do shit without having Yoshi nag him. As soon as she got in the car, Swerve raised up and wrapped his hands around Sharon's mouth. She tried to scream, but he squeezed tighter.

"Shut the fuck up, you conniving bitch!" he spat. "You were on some get back type shit, when you was the hoe, but watch how I get the last laugh," Swerve pulled the knife from his pocket and slit her throat.

She gurgled a little bit before taking her last breath. He grabbed her tips and left a beer bottle inside that he picked up off the ground to make it look like a normal robbery. Even though he had gloves on, Swerve was still sure to wipe everything he touched and then he got out of the car when he didn't see anymore. Thirty minutes later, Swerve walked into his condo. He took a long hot shower and hopped in the bed, smiling. One problem solved and Swerve laid there thinking about how he could handle the next one. The next morning, Swerve woke up feeling refreshed. He had sweet dreams about Rhapsodee and was more determined than ever to find her. She had changed her phone number and hadn't been posting in social media. Swerve knew that she was going to slip up sooner or later, and he was going to be right there to catch her. His phone rang and he knew it was a FaceTime call from Yoshi.

"Hey baby," he answered before the call went to voicemail.

"Hey love. You still in bed?"

"Yep, just relaxing. How y'all doing?"

"We're good. Just missing you. You know you gon' have to make up with my people, right? We can't have this tension," Yoshi pouted.

"In due time, but don't stress yourself out about that right now. It's all good baby."

They talked for a few minutes more until Yoshi's mom called her to come and eat breakfast. After saying their I love you's, Swerve got up and handled his hygiene and went to see if there was anything in the kitchen for him to eat, which he seriously doubted. Since Rhap had been gone, Swerve had pretty much been spending all of his time at Yoshi's and going grocery shopping for home hadn't been a priority. He had her thinking that he was all hers to ease her mind, but as soon as Rhap came back, he knew that he would be able to keep Yoshi in check because of all the time he had been giving her. When he didn't find shit, Swerve decided to go to iHop.

Swerve hadn't seen Leah since she moved his wife's things out of their place. He laid eyes on her when she was getting into her car and he had a good mind to snatch her ass up for fucking up his life, but another idea popped into his mind. Swerve hopped into his Challenger and headed towards his destination with a mind full of thoughts. All he needed was someone who was willing to make some money because he didn't need to get his hands dirty. When Swerve arrived, he went inside and placed an order for a Beef Tip and Hash Brown breakfast and scanned the restaurant.

The waitress brought Swerve his food piece by piece and thirty minutes later, he was done eating and standing in line to pay. A girl was in front of him and every card she pulled out was declined.

"Add her ticket to mine," Swerve stepped up and requested.

After he paid for the food, Swerve knew it was only a matter of time before the plan he had recently thought of would be into motion.

"I really appreciate you. Can I get your number so I can pay you back? I'm so embarrassed," the girl caught up to him and said.

"You don't have to worry about paying me back. Would you be interested in making a quick ten grand?"

"Ten thousand dollars? Hell yeah," the girl exclaimed.

"What kinda car you drive?" Swerve quizzed and the girl pointed to a Buick LeSabre. "Perfect," Swerve said and then led the girl to his car so that he could discuss the details in private.

After thirty minutes and a lot of convincing, Swerve headed to his safe to retrieve half of the money and he would withdraw the rest bright and early Monday morning. He allowed his partner in crime to follow him home and pick up the money. Once that was done, Swerve prayed that she could get the job done that day and all he had to do was play the waiting game. Swerve went back inside, grabbed a Heineken and then turned the TV on. He was about to turn to ESPN, but a breaking news story caught his attention.

"This is Brittany, reporting live from Dudley's, a local club here in the Atlanta area. During the early hours, one of the bartenders was found stabbed in her vehicle. The victim died, but video surveillance has been retrieved from the bar and the police are searching for an Africa American male between the age of twenty-five to thirty who drives a...."

Swerve turned the TV off because he didn't want to hear anymore. He had no idea that cameras were outside of the car and his heart sank. Paranoia set in instantly and he knew that he had to get to Yoshi's apartment.

At that very moment, he was so thankful for it and her because no one knew Yoshi and that was going to be his hiding place. Swerve knew that he had to ditch his car and lay all the way low.

Von Wiley Hall

Chapter Forty-Seven

Ever since finding out that she was having twins, E-Love had been on Leah's ass like white on rice. Even though she didn't want to be considered helpless, Leah had to admit that she was loving the attention that she was receiving from her man. For the past few weeks, Leah had been feeling like she was being followed. She had also missed being in a couple of accidents by missing a couple of exits. Shit was strange and she had no idea why, but when she told E-Love, he demanded that she work from home and assured her that he would run all her errands. Staying in the house had been once hell of a challenge, and Leah was happy that she was finally about to get out for her baby shower. Her phone rang and she saw that it was her cousin calling, which meant that she had to be outside.

"I'm unlocking the door now," Leah said as soon as she answered and then made her way to the front door.

"Happy Birthday!!! I'm so happy to see you! I'm so glad you made it!" Leah exclaimed, pulling Rhap as far as she could for a hug.

"Thank you!!! I'm happy to see you too and you know I wasn't missing this for nothing," Rhap replied.

Leah finally let her go and pulled her inside. They headed to the living room and sat down for some girl talk. Leah knew that her cousin wanted to be more hands on with the baby shower, but she demanded that she allow Twin and Princess to hold it down so that she could stay off the radar. They were getting things together at the moment and Leah was excited to see how everything was going to turn out.

"Sooo you gotta tell me all about Black. You done broke down and gave that man some yet?"

"Girrll, I really tried yo hold out, but I couldn't now that nigga got me sprung. I thought Swerve was good but whew!" Rhap said.

"That's what I'm talking about. How Black done put a stamp on it, so I ain't gotta worry 'bout t you tryna backtrack and shit. By the way, has Swerve contacted you on any social media or through email?

"You know he emailed me like crazy at first, but the past month, I haven't heard a thing so hopefully he gets the hint. I haven't been on social media. I had the divorce papers drawn up and sent out, but he hasn't been home to sign for them, so I don't know what's going on. It's actually kinda scary because Swerve isn't quiet unless something is wrong," Rhap explained.

"Well, let's just hope somebody else got his ass in line, so you can continue being free. Now, why did you pick this weekend to have my baby shower? You should have used that trip you planned as a getaway for you and Black. I know you wanted everything to be special, for you and Swerve on your birthday and anniversary, but he didn't deserve you love anyway."

"I just wanted to shake the weekend up with something happy, so now when September 1st rolls around I'll always remember that we celebrated our little babies instead of …him," Rhap shrugged.

"Well okay, let's get ready so we can be on time. All I gotta do is slip on my dress," Leah said, finally getting up after rocking back and forth a couple of times.

"You think you gon' make it to your due date?"

"Girl, I don't even know, but I got a feeling I will. If I do, that means my damn birthday trips gon' be over. At least for a couple of years," Leah rolled her eyes.

"You're so damn dramatic," Rhap laughed.

Twenty minutes later, Leah was dressed in a white dress and a pair of gold Jimmy Choo heels. The girls insisted that she dress in white and gold, and Rhap made sure it happened by purchasing everything herself.

"Aww you look so pretty. Did Stacey do your hair yesterday?"

"Yep she put me back in the game," Leah twirled around.

The shower was scheduled to start at four o'clock and Leah pulled into the venue that they rented at a quarter til. Rhap suggested that Leah drive because they would need an extra vehicle to help transport. Leah applied some more lip gloss before she got out. There were several cars there. Most she knew, but there were several that she didn't know. Before Leah could open her door, Twin was opening it and Princess was right behind her.

"Heyyy trick! Hey TT's babies," Twin hugged her rubbing on her stomach, talking to the unborn children.

"Hey girl hey!" Leah spoke to her friends and cousin.

"You look good Leah," Princess told her.

"Thank you and thank y'all so much for all of this," Leah got emotional.

"Girl we got you."

"No thanks needed."

"Stop that crying," each of them replied.

Leah got herself together and then made her way inside behind her friends. She was in awe at the sight before her. The color theme was pink, blue, gold and white. The center pieces were different on each table. Some were pictures of Leah and E-Love, some were pictures of the sonogram, others were little babies dressed in pink and blue. Leah was too emotional to take everything, but she saw a photographer and knew that she would have memories to always look back on. The room was full of people. E-Love's mom and sister were in attendance, some of her classmates from college and high school as well as old coworkers. Her crew knew everyone she dealt with, and it was apparent that they contacted every damn body. Leah's eyes landed on the food table and cakes and she couldn't stop herself from going to take a look. The fruit arrangement looked so beautiful and delicious that Leah was scared that she wasn't going to want anyone to touch it. That thought quickly left her mind when she reached and grabbed a grape through.

"Damn trick, this pregnancy is really showing your hungry side. Your little skinny ass, well not so much right now, can put down some food. Girl come on here, we gon' let you and the babies eat in a minute," Twin playfully popped her hand.

Twin, Princess and Rhap took turns hosting about five games and they ate. Leah stuffed her plate with crab legs, shrimp, potatoes, and corn. The fact that they had her favorite foods was enough to love them forever. After everyone stuffed their faces, Leah opened her gifts and was once again overwhelmed with the outpour of love. E-Love's mom and sister and her friends must have secretly been in competition with each other because they went all out. It took Leah almost two hours to open her gifts and surprisingly no one left. Leah stood up and gave her speech of thanks. Before she finished, E-Love walked in and he was followed by a few of his boys. Leah was happy to see them because that meant that they could load up everything and take it home.

Let's Get Married by Jagged Edge began to play. Leah didn't think anything of it until she turned around and saw E-Love on one knee in front of her. Her hands instantly covered her mouth and tears streamed down her cheeks. What was even crazier, E-love was singing right along with Jagged Edge and was actually holding a decent tune. He opened a black box and the rock that was before Leah caused her eyes to get as big as a silver dollar.

"Leah Chanel Fuquay, no one has ever made me feel like you have. I loved you before I even had the balls to admit it to you or myself. You've had my back since I've known you. When you should have walked away and left my ass alone, you stayed right there and none of your sacrifices have gone in vain. I admire your ambition and your strength, things that have made some people break, have only made you stronger. I can't imagine my life without having you by my side. Will you do me the honor of being my wife?"

"E-Love baby. Dayum you, nigga. Got me crying and shit. Of course, I will marry your crazy ass!" Leah sobbed and the room erupted in applause.

An hour later, E-Love and his boys had their vehicles loaded with the gifts and everyone was gone except close family and friends.

"Now it's time for you to get my grandbabies here," Jonetta beamed.

"Eight more weeks. Time has really been flying by," Leah rubbed her belly. "Okay, so who is coming to the house to help me put up these gifts?" Rhap queried and everyone she expected to help agreed.

Each of them piled into their vehicles and headed towards E-Love's house. Right when Leah exited the venue and got on the highway, she felt a big bang, causing her car to emerge out into traffic. When she looked out of her window, she saw an eighteen-wheeler coming her way and all she could do was close her eyes and scream.

Von Wiley Hall

Chapter Forty-Eight

Swerve was laying on the couch depressed as hell. It was Rhap's birthday and also their anniversary and he still had no idea where she was. He had been messaging her on all social media sites, but she never even opened the messages. He really wished that he could turn back the hands of time and do things a little different. Swerve had been cooped up in the house for the past month, making sure he wasn't noticed by anyone. To say he was scared shitless would have been an understatement. He was pissed at himself that he didn't do enough research to find out there were cameras outside of the bar.

"Come on Swerve!' Yoshi yelled out.

"I told you, I don't wanna go out unless it's absolutely necessary," he grumbled.

"I think having this baby is necessary!" Yoshi screamed and Swerve jumped up.

"You're having the baby? Oh my God. Got damn! Shit! He paced the floor.

"Swerve, get it together! My fuckin' water just broke and you acting like you in labor!' Yoshi screamed.

"Mommy, you're about to have the baby?" J.J. excitedly hollered.

"Yes baby!" Yoshi managed to say between her deep breaths.

"Okay, let me grab your bag and then we can head out. I got you," Swerve tried to convince himself. He was nervous as fuck. They still didn't know what they were having because the baby's legs were always closed, but it appeared that they would know soon. Swerve couldn't fool himself any longer, he was excited as hell about his family, but he still wanted Rhap. He forced himself to push thoughts of her to the back of her mind so that he could be there for Yoshi.

It seemed that every time he was in her presence and thinking of Rhap, Yoshi knew, and he needed her mind on delivering his baby at that moment. Five minutes later, they were in the car on their way to North DeKalb Medical Center. Swerve had the blinkers on, weaving in and out of traffic. He tried to remain calm with Yoshi in the passenger seat, screaming and was a nervous wreck. After almost wrecking about two times, Swerve finally made it to the hospital and double parked near the emergency entrance.

Everything happened too damn fast for Swerve to keep up with. Yoshi was taken to labor and delivery and he heard one of the nurses say that she had dilated five centimeters. They kept coming into the room to check every few minutes and she asked them for an epidural. Swerve was happy as hell when it kicked in because she stopped cussing him out so much. J.J. was in the corner playing his PS4 and Swerve had a moment to really think. He was really about to have a baby on his wife's birthday and their anniversary. Thoughts of letting Rhap go and being with Yoshi plagued his mind, but he felt conflicted.

A few hours later, he heard the nurse saying it was time to push. He stood by Yoshi's side after J.J. was escorted to the nursery waiting room where Yoshi's mom was waiting. Swerve didn't even think to call her, but Yoshi texted her when her water broke. Less than twenty minutes later, Yoshi pushed out a baby boy, but Swerve told her that she was going to have a little girl. They both smiled when they looked at their baby. After they cleaned him up, they both held him for a few minutes until Yoshi drifted off to sleep. The nurse told Swerve she had to take the baby to the nursery for a while and that he was welcome to follow her.

When Yoshi drifted off to sleep, Swerve decided to head to the waiting room to get his son so that he could see his baby brother. Swerve went and spoke to Yoshi's mom and then grabbed J.J.'s hands. Before he went to the nursery, he thought about the fact that he had double parked and then did a light jog remembering where he parked. His car was nowhere in sight and Swerve panicked. Not only because he knew that it had been towed, but because he knew that they were going to run his plates and match his car to the murder scene.

"Fuck!" he swore and them made his way back inside.

"Daddy, can I see my little brother?" J.J. asked.

"Yeah son, we 'bout to head that way now."

"Ain't that Swerve?"

"And didn't that lil boy say daddy?"

Swerve heard some voices say those words and that caused him to stop in his tracks. When he turned around, Swerve came face to face with Rhap, visibly staring at him and his son. All of the thoughts about letting her go were long gone and something fresh popped into his mind.

Von Wiley Hall

Hard and Ruthless

Chapter Forty-Nine

Rhap's heart dropped when the scene unfolded right before her eyes. It was almost as if the girl purposely ran into Leah. When Leah's car swerved one last time, the impact from the truck hit the other car head on. When her car came to a stop and the coast was clear, Rhap jumped out of her car and ran towards her cousin.

E-Love and Black had already left, and it wasn't on her mind to call them. Everything happened so fast. How did a perfect day turn upside down so quickly? Rhap, along with Princess, Twin and the others were all 'bout to leave ran towards the accident scene at the same time. There was an ambulance nearby and they turned on their sirens and blocked traffic before Rhap could cross the street.

When she made it, it looked like Leah's head was lying to the side, but Rhap couldn't get any closer because a paramedic stopped her. Three cop cars pulled up simultaneously and blocked the pathway for everyone.

"That's my cousin. She's pregnant. I gotta make sure she's okay!" Rhap screamed as tears ran down her face.

"Do you know who her doctor is? That'll help us get her to the right hospital," one of the EMT's asked Rhap.

She gave them the info and then decided to head to the hospital because they wasted no time putting Leah in the back of the ambulance. Rhap noticed that the cops were leaning over the girl who had been hit by the truck with a notepad.

She couldn't worry about that at the moment, she had to make sure her cousin was okay. After she hopped back in her car, she instantly called Black, but he didn't answer. So, then she called E-Love and he didn't answer. She figured that they must have made it home and were unloading the gifts. She sent them both a text and told them to get to North Dekalb Medical Center ASAP.

Rhap arrived at the hospital twenty minutes later. She parked and got out in a hurry. Out of the corner of her eye, she thought she saw Swerve's car parked wrong, but she didn't have time to stop and investigate the tag number. Rhap knew that it was too soon to get information on her cousin, but she tried anyway.

"Hey, my cousin was just brought in. How is she?"

"What's her name?"

"Leah Fuquay."

"She is in the system, but there aren't any updates. If you'll take a seat, we'll be sure to update you as soon as we can," the receptionist told her.

Rhap knew there wasn't anything she could do at the moment. By the time she made her way to the waiting area, everyone else was walking through the doors. She updated them on what the receptionist had told her, and they shocked the hell out of her with some news of their own. The lady who hit Leah told the officers that she was paid by a James St. John to crash into the lady, but the woman died right before she was placed in the ambulance and before she could tell them anything else. Twin advised Rhapsodee that the cops had the lady's phone and would be checking into things, and they also informed them that Swerve's name was already on their radar as a murder suspect. Rhap couldn't believe her ears, but Swerve had been a completely different person for the past few months, so she couldn't defend him at all.

Everyone sat around quiet for a few minutes, and then Rhap decided to find a vending machine so that she could get a bottle of water. Twin and Princess got up and followed, each of them getting a bottle of Dasani.

"Man, this is so fucked up. But I think, no I know she's gonna be okay y'all. We just gotta be positive," Twin broke the silence as they stood by the vending machines.

"I think so too," Princess agreed.

Before Rhap could respond to them, her phone started ringing and it was Black. She briefed him on what happened and told him that him and E-Love were on the way. They made their way back towards the waiting room and Rhap bumped into Twin because she had stopped in her tracks.

"Daddy can I see my little brother?" a little boy asked.

"Yeah son, we 'bout to head that way now."

"Ain't that Swerve?" Twin asked.

"And didn't that lil boy say daddy?" Princess chimed in.

Hard and Ruthless

Rhap stared at Swerve and he finally locked eyes with her. She looked between him and the little boy and there was no denying that the duo were father and son. Rhap wanted to say something, but her words were caught in her throat. She wasn't completely over Swerve, but the total disrespect had Rhap wanting to fuck him up.

"Baby, I've been looking all over for you. Happy Birthday and Happy Anniversary. I'm sorry for everything. I didn't mean for everything to go down the way that it did. Please forgive me," Swerve walked towards her, pleading his case and trying to pull her into his arms like everything was gravy.

"Don't you fuckin' touch me ever again!' she spat.

"You're still my wife and you gon' respect me!" Swerve grabbed her arm harshly and yanked her, forgetting that they were in a hospital and that his son was with him.

"Oh, hell naw, bitch! You've put your hands on her for the last time," Twin asserted before Twin and Princess both landed blows on him and then Rhap joined in.

The only thing that stopped Rhap was the little boy crying. No matter how she felt about Swerve, the child was innocent. She finally was able to raise her voice and got Twin and Princess to calm down when a few people walked in the area that they were occupying. Once they were gone, Swerve grabbed Rhap's arm again and tried to explain himself.

"Look baby, it's not what you think. He was born before we got together, and I just found out about him a couple of months ago.

"Swerve let me the fuck go! I don't give a damn anymore. You've ruined my life enough and you're outta chances. We just heard that you're a murder suspect and you paid someone to make Leah have an accident. You think I wanna be with you after you tried to kill my cousin? Get the fuck outta here."

"Listen to me, Rhap!"

"Nigga if you don't get yo bitch ass hands off her right fuckin' now!"

Von Wiley Hall

Chapter Fifty

Black made his way toward Rhapsodee and Swerve, ready to attack. When he saw the grip that Swerve had on Rhap's arm, he didn't see shit but red. He already had it out for the nigga and for him walkin' in on that scene only added fuel to his fire. By the time Black and E-Love made it to them, so did two police officers and a couple of staff members who had been lurking in the shadows.

"I've been waiting to see you," Black snatched Swerve up.

"Wait baby, don't do anything crazy," Rhap grabbed Black's arm.

"Baby? You're calling this thug ass nigga baby right in front of my face?" Swerve finally found his voice.

"Swerve cut the shit. You know it's over!"

"Do we have a problem here?" one of the officers intervened.

"Hell no," came from Black while Rhap, Princess, and Twin screamed, "Hell yeah,"

Princess took that moment to fill the cops in on everything that they had learned about Swerve. One of the cops stepped away and made a phone call.

"Family of Leah Fuquay," a nurse called out and that pulled E-Love and Twin away from the current scene, leading them to the area that Leah was located. Rhap and Princess stood still along with Black.

Swerve grabbed the little boy's arm and tried to walk away, but the officer stopped him.

"Stand still sir!" he commanded.

"James St. John, you're under arrest for the murder of Sharon Jackson-Perez. You have the right to remain silent, anything you say can and will be used in a court of law. You have the right to an attorney…"

"Get off of me! How y'all arrest me over some bullshit in front of my son?" Swerve argued and the little boy started crying. "J.J., go back to labor and delivery and stay with your grandma," Swerve instructed, and the little boy took off running. After overhearing

what the man said, a nurse caught up with J.J. and took him to labor and delivery, ensuring that he didn't got lost and got to his grandma
Black was pissed off that he couldn't handle Swerve the way that he wanted to handle him.

"You are over that nigga, right?" Black turned around and asked Rhap.

"Of course, I am, but I don't want you doing anything to get in any trouble baby. Let the law handle him, okay?"

Black pondered over what Rhap said. He had fallen in love with her and would do anything for her, but he wasn't sure if his pride and need to protect her would allow him to let that shit slide.

"Baby, please just promise me that you won't put your hands on him," Rhap said.

"Okay, I promise I won't put my hands on him," Black agreed.

"You know what I mean," Rhap challenged.

"I'm a man of my word baby. I won't do shit to him," he told her.

"Okay, let's go check on Leah." No one could believe the events of the day had turned out. When they rounded the corner, they saw Twin standing outside of Leah's room, crying, and Black's mind began to think the worse.

Chapter Fifty-One

E-Love wanted to kill that bitch ass nigga, Swerve, but he had to check on his fiancée and make sure that her and the babies were fine. The nurse led E-Love to Leah's room and his heart was beating fast as fuck. He knew he didn't talk to God as often as he should, but he prayed with each step that he took. E-Love blamed himself for not protecting her and he wasn't sure if he would be able to live with himself if something bad happened. When he entered the room, Leah was sitting up in the bed, fussing at one of the other nurses.

"I'm fine. I just wanna go home and put our babies gifts up."

E-Love rushed over to her bedside and pulled her in for a hug.

"Baby you okay?"

"Yeah, I feel fine baby, but they're saying I gotta stay overnight I got a slight concussion or something."

"The babies?" E-Love nervously asked.

"The babies are fine, sir. We just have to keep them overnight for observations. It's standard. A lot of mothers of twins don't go full term so we have to be extra careful," the nurse explained.

"Thank God," E-Love hugged his girl again. "Now Leah, you gotta relax and do what they say. I'll be right here with you," E-Love comforted her.

"You gon' stay here all night?"

"Fa sho. Let me go and let everybody know you okay though," E-Love kissed her and then made his way outside of her room, where he left Twin in the hallway.

He should have known that his mom would find her way where they were.

When he closed her door, he saw Twin crying and wondered what was going on.

"Twin stop thinking the worst. We don't even know who that nurse was talking about," he heard his mom saying to Leah's friend as Rhap and Black walked up.

"What's going on?" E-Love asked, getting the attention of everyone.

"Is she okay?"

217

"E-Love, how is she and the babies?

"What did the doctor say?

Everyone fired off question after question after question. E-Love filled them in on everything and then all of the women rushed off to see Leah. He stayed back so he could holla at his bruh. They chopped it up about the entire situation and agreed that they had to fall back for a little while just to keep the heat off them. E-Love listened as Black shared a few thoughts and he nodded his head in agreement. E-Love and Black made their way back to the room and could hear laughter before they opened the door. The glow that was on Leah's face made E-Love's heart melt. He was happy with the choice he made to put a ring on her finger, but suddenly he felt that wasn't enough. Another idea popped up into E-Love's head and he hoped that Leah would agree with him.

The next morning, E-Love woke up and stared down at his fiancée. She must have felt his presence because she stirred a little and then looked back at him.

"I want you to have my last name before our kids get here," E-Love expressed.

"Who are you and where is my man?" Leah chuckled.

"I'm for real. Let's get married today!"

"You serious?" she wondered because she was beyond ready.

"Dead ass. I'm ready for you to be my wife."

E-Love knew that Leah was who he wanted to spend the rest of his life with. There weren't any skeletons in his closet. He has even handled the Mya situation before could get started. Leah was all he wanted and needed.

"Okay. Alrighty then. Let's do it," she smiled and kissed him with all she had.

After calling and telling their people about the impromptu wedding, E-Love sent her girls on a mission to make the day one to remember.

Once Twin and Princess arrived at the hospital with everything that E-Love had requested, they both showered and waited for the official discharge papers. Leaving the hospital, E-Love sent his mom a text and let her know what was going on. He also texted

Black and Bobby B to fill them in. The situation with Bobby B was handled and E-Love was happy as shit about that. Things were finally headed in the right direction. They arrived at the courthouse thirty minutes later, dressed in all black, E-Love's favorite color, and made things official.

Von Wiley Hall

Chapter Fifty-Two

Swerve headed to the shower, when he felt like everyone was done. He couldn't believe what his life had become. If he could turn back the hands of time, he would do so in a heartbeat. When he got arrested at the hospital, he was never granted bail and had to sit in jail until his court date, which was scheduled for the second week in January. Swerve had only laid eyes on Yoshi and his newborn once since then. She visited him and let him know that she was moving back to Kentucky with her mom. Swerve couldn't ask her to stay by his side. Swerve still refused to sign the divorce papers. No matter what, his heart wouldn't allow him to do so.

He took a lukewarm shower and soon as he cut the water off, he turned around and bumped into the dude they called Alex.

"You need this shower man? I'm done" Swerve tried to step around him.

"Nah, got a message for ya though. Black and E-Love said rest in hell," Alex said and then stabbed Swerve in the throat.

Swerve plummeted to the floor. Feeling the water come back on, he laid there in the shower with the water running on him while he fought for his last breath.

To Be Continued...
Hard and Ruthless 2
Coming Soon

Submission Guideline

Submit the first three chapters of your completed manuscript to ldpsubmissions@gmail.com, subject line: Your book's title. The manuscript must be in a .doc file and sent as an attachment. Document should be in Times New Roman, double spaced and in size 12 font. Also, provide your synopsis and full contact information. If sending multiple submissions, they must each be in a separate email.

Have a story but no way to send it electronically? You can still submit to LDP/Ca$h Presents. Send in the first three chapters, written or typed, of your completed manuscript to:

LDP: Submissions Dept
Po Box 944
Stockbridge, Ga 30281

DO NOT send original manuscript. Must be a duplicate.

Provide your synopsis and a cover letter containing your full contact information.

Thanks for considering LDP and Ca$h Presents.